M. N.

D0835857

Six-shooter Bride

Slammed in a jail cell after killing a man in a crooked poker game, Ethan Craig's future looks bleak. Then a witness, Amelia Ash, comes forward and offers Ethan a way out. But there's a catch. Amelia needs someone to escort her on a treacherous journey across bandit-infested country to her forthcoming wedding.

Ethan agrees to take her, but with raging rivers to cross and Buck Lincoln's outlaw gang on her tail, it isn't long before he realizes just how treacherous this journey will be. There's danger every step of the way in this gripping western.

Six-shooter Bride

I. J. Parnham

A Black Horse Western

ROBERT HALE · LONDON

© I. J. Parnham 2005
First published in Great Britain 2005

ISBN 0 7090 7835 8

Robert Hale Limited
Clerkenwell House
Clerkenwell Green
London EC1R 0HT

976, 888 / ALF

Typeset by
Derek Doyle & Associates, Shaw Heath.
Printed and bound in Great Britain by
Antony Rowe Limited, Wiltshire

CHAPTER 1

Leach Oldrich was fingering his whiskey glass again, and that meant he couldn't have a straight flush. And Ethan Craig reckoned he'd risk his last dollar to prove it.

Trouble was, it really was his last dollar, and Leach knew it.

One last time Ethan glanced at his four displayed cards: two jacks, a three and a queen, then lifted the corner of his hidden queen. He glanced at Leach's hand: the four, five, six and eight of hearts. Then he looked up at Leach, but Leach met his gaze with a steady eye.

And for Ethan, that clinched it.

'I'll pay to see what you've got.' Ethan threw his stake into the pot. 'And you just ain't got a straight or a flush.'

Leach chuckled. 'And I'm looking forward to taking your money.'

Ethan leaned forward. 'And I was right. You're just too confident.'

Leach pursed his lips, then sipped his whiskey,

prolonging the moment before he revealed his hand. As he placed the glass down, his lips curled with a slight smile and, for just for a moment, doubt invaded Ethan's mind, but then Leach snorted and tipped his hidden card over.

It was the queen of clubs, and he had a nothing hand.

Ethan leaned back, then tipped over his queen. Leach didn't even look at the card as he gestured for Ethan to take the pot. As the other players grunted their appreciation, Ethan pulled the bills towards him.

'And with that,' the rancher to Ethan's right said, 'I'm leaving.'

'Me, too,' the plump banker opposite Ethan said, patting his ample stomach. 'I got me a bank to open up before the good citizens of Lodesville start complaining.'

Leach pouted. 'But surely you gentlemen will give me a chance to win back my money.'

The banker stood. 'I'm up ten dollars, and that's good enough for me.'

'And I'm down five,' the rancher said. 'And that was good enough for me, too.'

'That mean neither of you is man enough to fight it out on another hand?'

The rancher glanced at the saloon doors, then placed both hands on the table and leaned forward to confront Leach.

'I can stay for another hand and teach you a lesson for that arrogance.'

The banker stared aloft, but then withdrew his

watch and glanced at it.

'And I suppose those customers can wait another few minutes,' he murmured with a resigned sigh.

And so Leach dealt another hand.

As he dealt Ethan glanced at Leach wondering, as he guessed everyone else around the table was, whether he was a bad player, or a good one. Leach's unsubtle taunt after his systematic losses of the last two hours was such an obvious way of raising the stakes and taking somebody for every last cent he had.

But sometimes the most obvious ways are the easiest ways to succeed.

With this in mind, Ethan guarded his profits and backed out of the hand before anyone became serious. And sure enough, everybody suddenly felt that Leach had dealt them their best hand in the last two hours and the stakes grew with nobody prepared to back out.

When all the cards were down, the banker had two pair displayed and a possible full house. Leach had three kings and a possible fourth. The rancher was sitting on three exposed queens and as he had shown no inclination to bluff, Ethan reckoned he just had to have a fourth.

Ethan leaned back, watching everyone and trying to deduce whether Leach had been cheating to manufacture this position. From the corner of his eye he saw him repeatedly finger his gunbelt, suggesting he might have secreted a card there, but, just as the stakes rose to fifty dollars, a shadow fell across the table.

7

Ethan glanced up, but to his surprise the newcomer was a woman. Ethan judged her to be in her earlier twenties. She wore a crisp and stern dress and despite her pleasing oval face sported an expression to match.

'Mr Oldrich,' she intoned, tapping a firm foot on the floor. 'You are already one hour late.'

'Amelia, stay outside like I told you to,' Leach murmured, not even looking up. 'And I'll join you just as soon as I've won my money back.'

'Based on your record of the last two days, I cannot wait that long. We will go now.'

Her comment dragged a round of laughter from the table. Leach murmured his irritation, but made no move to stand.

'I'll raise another ten dollars,' he said, favouring the banker with a firm glare.

Ethan glanced at Amelia, wondering if she was a part of Leach's routine. The distracting arrival of a flustered and comely young woman just as the stakes got high *was* mighty suspicious.

Amelia snorted her breath through her nostrils, then swung her head to the side to peer down at Ethan.

'And what are you looking at?' she demanded.

Ethan leaned back in his chair to appraise her from behind. 'The best view I've seen in many a year.'

Colour rose in her cheeks, but she firmed her jaw and looked away from Ethan as she folded her arms.

'Mr Oldrich, take me away from this . . . this place, immediately.'

Leach grunted his irritation and, with a few

glances at Amelia, another round of bets went into the pot. This proved too much for the banker and he folded, leaving just Leach and the rancher, who paid to see Leach's hand.

Leach glanced up at Amelia, winked, receiving a pout in response, then tipped over his hidden card. He had a full house, kings over tens.

The rancher and Leach shared eye contact. Then the rancher flipped over his final card to show that he did have four queens.

Leach blinked hard and delivered a pronounced gulp.

'You played well,' he murmured, nothing in his sullen tone suggesting that this was a compliment.

'And I hope you're happy with the result,' the rancher said, leaning back to edge his jacket aside and display the ivory handle of his gun. 'I don't want you to go thinking I cheated.'

Leach glanced at the gun.

'Nothing of the sort.'

'Then I'll collect.' The rancher moved forward, his gaze on Leach, but Ethan lunged and slapped a hand on his wrist.

'And I don't reckon you will,' he said.

The rancher swung his gaze from Leach to appraise Ethan. 'What you trying to say, friend?'

'I'm saying you just cheated.'

The rancher's right eye twitched.

'You weren't even in the game.'

'I wasn't, and that gave me plenty of time to watch what you were doing. And you just slipped yourself that queen from your sleeve.'

'You reckon you can prove it?'

'Perhaps not, but I can prove this.' Ethan raised his hand from the rancher's wrist then grabbed his jacket and threw it open. Tucked into the inside pocket was the four of hearts, which he threw, face up, on to the table.

As the rancher opened and closed his mouth soundlessly, Leach delivered a broad smile.

'Obliged for your observing skills, Ethan.'

'Don't be. Because he ain't the only one cheating here. You palmed that second ten several hands ago and I reckon if I investigate your clothes, I'll find the queen that this man just couldn't have.'

Leach's jaw muscles rippled, but then he smiled and exchanged a glance with the rancher.

'What you reckon?' he asked.

The rancher rubbed his jaw then gave a resigned shrug.

'Split the pot?'

'Hey,' the banker whined. 'I had a stake in that pot and I had a good hand. And all without cheating.'

For long moments everyone stared at everyone else. Then the banker thrust his hand to his holster. Ethan jumped back from the table, drawing his gun with his right hand and pushing Amelia to the floor with his left hand. But as he swung his gun round to aim at Leach the rancher drew and blasted lead sideways at the banker.

The shot caught him high on the shoulder and wheeled him to the floor. Before the rancher could fire again, Ethan planted a slug in his forehead that kicked him back in his chair. He tumbled to the floor to lie still seated in his upturned chair with his legs high.

Ethan swung his gun back to the table, covering Leach and the banker as he backed away two paces, but Leach thrust his hands high. The banker was writhing on the floor, clutching his shoulder. Ethan paced around the table to peer down at the rancher's body.

He confirmed that the rancher was dead; then noticed the quietness in the saloon. Everyone who was surrounding the table was looking behind him towards the saloon doors.

Ethan stood tall and glanced over his shoulder, but it was to see a man with a star and a Peacemaker levelled on him.

'I'm Sheriff Pye,' the man said, 'and you'll holster that gun, cowboy, or die where you stand.'

CHAPTER 2

'You got no right holding me in here,' Ethan shouted, slapping the cell bars.

Sheriff Pye stared at Ethan through the bars.

'I have strict rules on men who draw guns in my town,' he said, 'and you just broke every one of them.'

Ethan stood back from the bars and put on the most pleasant smile he could muster.

'But I'm no trouble. I only stepped in when those cheating poker-players were all set to start shooting each other.'

'Perhaps they were, or perhaps they weren't, but the only thing I know for sure is that Leach Oldrich ain't agreeing with your story.'

'Then ask the banker.'

'He's just had a slug removed from his shoulder and is out cold, and will be for a while.' The sheriff shrugged. 'Assuming he lives.'

Ethan looked away, sighing. 'But I'm an honest man. You can trust me.'

'Yeah, yeah,' the sheriff said, then yawned. 'And

when I've checked your story and proved you ain't spinning me a yarn, I'll let you go.'

'And how long will that be?'

The sheriff rubbed his bristled chin.

'How long do you reckon it'll take me to check out a story as unlikely as yours?'

Ethan slumped down on to his bunk.

'I'll get comfortable.'

'You do that because I reckon . . .' The sheriff glanced over his shoulder as the door creaked open. He tipped back his hat as Amelia, the woman from the saloon, paced into the office, then raised his hat. 'And what can I do for you, ma'am?'

'I have relevant information on that man in the cell,' she said, pointing at Ethan.

For his part, Ethan jumped up and punched the air.

'Much obliged, ma'am,' Ethan said as he stood on the boardwalk. He rose on his heels and threw back his arms as he drew in an exaggerated breath of air.

'That is quite all right,' Amelia said, looking into the road. 'But I was a witness and I only told Sheriff Pye what I saw.'

'Can't say I ain't surprised that you spoke up for me. I thought Leach was with you.'

She shivered. 'My uncle had hired Mr Oldrich to escort me to White Creek and ensure that I come to no harm on the way, but he is a hard-drinking and raucous man, and I have been finding his company increasingly disagreeable. So, I have dispensed with his services.'

Ethan nodded. 'Why go to a place like that?'

'On Friday, I am to be wed. And so I am now in need of someone else to escort me to White Creek.'

Ethan narrowed his eyes, then shrugged and looked away.

'Then I wish you luck.'

She swung round to stand before Ethan and smiled. Ethan couldn't help but flinch when he noticed for the first time just how white her teeth were and that her eyes were the deepest blue he had ever seen.

'But I was hoping I could employ you,' she said, lowering her voice.

'Ma'am, you seem a right pleasant young woman, and I got to tell you the truth.' Ethan set his hands on his hips. 'I ain't much different to Leach. I like a drink, and I can get raucous when I feel in the mood.'

'Perhaps you do, but I believe myself to be a good judge of character, and I reckon you are a good man at heart. Mr Oldrich was not.'

'Obliged. But White Creek is a few hundred miles that-a-way.' Ethan pointed as he paced out from the boardwalk, then swung his hand over his shoulder to point in the opposite direction. 'And I'm heading that-a-way.'

'Then I thank you for considering my request.' She turned to the sheriff's office, then turned back and raised a hand. 'Please stay there.'

Ethan paced back on to the boardwalk and set his feet wide.

'Why?'

14

'To ensure that Sheriff Pye doesn't have to search too far for you.' She raised a hand to the door.

'Whoa!' Ethan shouted, halting Amelia as her fingers brushed the handle. 'Are you saying that you're going in there to take back your story because I won't escort you to White Creek?'

A smile twitched the corners of her mouth.

'I judged your character correctly. You are not only a man who champions fairness, but a man who is endowed with uncommon intelligence.'

Ethan sighed and looked skywards.

'How much will you pay me for this . . . this inconvenient journey?'

'I will pay you one dollar a day, including today, with a bonus of another dollar if you get me to White Creek safely by Friday.'

'You expect me to accept six dollars,' Ethan muttered, waving his hands above his head, 'to go about seven hundred miles out of my way?'

'Five dollars. You must get me to White Creek *by* Friday.'

Ethan sighed. 'This offer just keeps on getting better and better.'

'So,' Ethan asked, 'what's the name of your betrothed?'

'Wesley Lister,' Amelia said with pride in her voice, as if Ethan should have heard of and been impressed by this person.

They were thirty miles down the trail from Lodesville. Amelia rode a piebald with an accomplished grace that had already made Ethan adjust downwards the time it would take them to reach White Creek.

'And have you been sweethearts for long?'

'Why all the questions?'

'Hey, I'm just passing the time,' Ethan said, raising his hands. 'We'll be riding together for a while and I don't like the thought of being quiet all the time.'

'I guess that is right. Wesley and I were, as you say, sweethearts, but we were too young to wed. And when we were old enough, my father became ill and . . . and my brother died in a fire. I requested to go to Bolt Gorge to study at Mrs Haversham's school for young ladies. And now that I have graduated, I am returning to wed.'

Ethan mouthed numbers to himself. 'And you haven't seen your sweetheart in all those years?'

'No, but we have corresponded on a regular basis, and I understand from his letters that his feelings haven't changed, so we are to be wed.'

'From letters!' Ethan snorted. 'You can't judge someone from words.'

Amelia raised her chin as she glanced at Ethan.

'I take from that comment that you cannot read.'

'Ain't had much need for it.'

'Schooling lets everyone achieve their full potential.'

'Does it?' Ethan swung round in the saddle to consider Amelia. 'And this Leach, was he good with books and suchlike?'

'I believe that was one of his few graces.'

'Then he's just gone even further down in my estimation because I don't exactly understand the route

16

you've taken to get here.' Ethan pulled his horse to a halt and outlined Amelia's route with an outstretched finger. 'You left Bolt Gorge and headed south to Lodesville. And now we have to head up to the ferry at Bear Pass then get the train at Green Valley, which will take us to White Creek.'

'That is our route.'

'Well, if I were escorting a young woman such as yourself, I'd have headed west from Bolt Gorge and boarded the train at Restitution.'

'That was more than one hundred miles out of our way.'

'It was, but then you could have travelled for most of the way on the train and arrived far more composed.'

Amelia glanced over her shoulder, then sniffed.

'Perhaps you should ask Mr Oldrich why he chose that route. He's following us. And I would have hoped that my protector would have known he was approaching and not be so concerned with offering unwanted criticism.'

'I know he's following us. He's 200 yards back and will meet us at . . .' Ethan rose in the saddle to glance forwards. '. . . at that creek.'

'How do you know that? You never even looked back.'

Ethan tugged on the reins and moved off.

'I didn't learn how to see backwards while riding forwards in no book of learning I can tell you. Now, do you want to break there and talk with Leach, or not?'

Amelia bristled but hurried on to join him and,

with another glance back, she shivered.

'Yes to the first question. No the second.'

They rode on to stop by the creek, and while Amelia watered and fed their horses, Ethan stood on the trail facing the oncoming Leach.

'You folks mind if I ride along with you?' Leach asked, pulling his horse to a halt, ten yards back. Ethan set his hands on his hips.

'You got some nerve asking that after you didn't speak up for me.'

'And you,' Amelia shouted from the bank of the creek, 'are no longer in my employ.'

'So you've said,' Leach shouted, looking over Ethan's shoulder, 'but your uncle paid me two hundred dollars to ensure you—'

'*Two* hundred dollars!' Ethan shouted.

'Yeah, it was a fair rate to protect his favourite niece.' Leach laughed as he looked at the exasperated Ethan. 'How much is she paying you?'

Ethan stood tall and forced the shock from his face with a sharp bite of his bottom lip.

'That's between Amelia and me.' He coughed and put on his best poker face. 'And it sure is a better deal than you got.'

Leach narrowed his eyes as he peered down at Ethan.

'Better? I doubt it. She has no money at the moment.'

Amelia pouted. 'This debate is irrelevant. You have not completed your side of the deal, and my uncle has no need to pay you.'

'Now, ma'am, you got no say in whatever deals

your uncle and me have agreed. And he'll pay me whether you ride with me or not.'

Amelia opened her mouth to argue, but with a determined swing of her skirt she knelt beside the creek and dangled a kerchief in the water, then patted her brow with it.

Ethan watched Leach smile, then gestured down the trail.

'You just ain't welcome here. You should ride on.'

'And there ain't no point in us trying to avoid each other.' Leach raised a hand and waved it beside the other hand. 'We're heading to the same place and we'll end up passing each other again and again and again.'

As Ethan rubbed his chin, peering away from Leach, Amelia joined him and shook her head.

'Then we'll keep on passing each other,' she said, 'because I don't want you riding with me.'

Leach stared down at Amelia, his thin lips curling with disapproval, then looked at Ethan. In turn, Amelia also looked at Ethan, her eyebrows raised in what Ethan took to be a request for support, but Ethan shrugged.

'I got no objection to you joining us,' he said, then raised his voice as Amelia stamped her foot and bleated her objection. 'Just don't get in the way, and don't expect us to wait around for you.'

As Leach tipped his hat, Amelia paced round to stand before Ethan.

'Mr Craig,' she snapped, 'I must object.'

'Object all you like, but Leach's joining us.' Ethan headed to his horse. 'And we're moving on straight away.'

Amelia hurried after him. 'But why let that . . . that . . . man come with us? He's the least trustworthy man I've ever had the misfortune to meet.'

Ethan stopped beside his horse. He glanced over his shoulder to confirm that Leach was out of earshot, then turned to Amelia.

'He's staying with us *because* he is so untrustworthy.' Ethan winked. 'Because then, I can keep an eye on him.'

CHAPTER 3

Throughout a sultry afternoon, the three riders rode on towards Bear Pass, the first stopping place on their journey to White Creek. The settlement was spread over both sides of the easiest crossing point within one hundred miles along the River Green. Although Ethan had never been there, he expected to find somewhere to stay for the night which would be suitable for him and his charge.

Ethan took the lead, with Amelia riding two horse lengths behind him. Leach brought up the rear. Since Leach had joined them, Amelia and Ethan had remained silent.

But when they reached Tarrat's Gorge, the winding and narrow approach to Bear Pass, Ethan leaned back to shout brief orders to Amelia and Leach to head towards a pass to their side then skirt around the gorge.

Amelia accepted this redirection without comment, but Leach nudged his horse forward to join Ethan.

'Why go that way?' Leach asked. 'It'll take an hour

through the gorge, but this detour will take at least two.'

'It might, but I've heard the gorge is riddled with rattlers.' Ethan turned to glance at Leach. 'And some bigger kinds of snake.'

'You get snakes everywhere, but there ain't no bandits there now. Bear Pass prospers by looking after the travellers who use the ferry, and that means the route is well patrolled.'

'You may be right.' Ethan smiled. 'But I trust my instincts. And as Amelia is paying me to use those instincts, we'll avoid the gorge.'

'This is ridiculous.' Leach glanced at Amelia, but if he was hoping for support, she rebuffed him with a curt refusal.

Ethan chuckled. 'If you're that concerned, you don't have to come with us. You can get there first and reserve us a room.'

'Rooms,' Amelia murmured.

As Leach glanced around, shrugging, Ethan urged his horse on ahead. Amelia hurried on to join him.

Leach muttered his displeasure, but then trotted after them. Amelia glanced back at him, then glanced at Ethan, but Ethan didn't give Leach any opportunity to complain again and stayed looking forward.

For the next half-hour Leach followed them quietly, but when they emerged from the pass and another pass that arced away from the gorge confronted them, he joined them and restarted questioning Ethan's decision to take this detour.

This time, Ethan let him complain, even encouraging him to explain himself, but he made no move to veer towards the gorge.

But as they rode into the short pass, he pulled his horse to a halt. He peered down the pass, then at the lowering sun, then leaned back to look towards the gorge. He rubbed his chin, then nodded.

'Perhaps you're right,' he said.

'At last,' Leach snapped, raising his hands high then slapping his legs. 'There's a turning about a half-mile back.'

'Lead on.' Ethan held his hand to the side, directing Leach to turn.

Leach swung his horse around, muttering about all the time they'd wasted, but when his back was to Ethan, Ethan drew his gun and aimed it squarely at the centre of Leach's back.

Amelia's mouth fell open, a strangulated squeal escaping her lips.

Leach glanced over his shoulder at her, but on noticing she wasn't moving, looked at Ethan, then at the gun. He flinched.

'What you done that for?'

'You will dismount, keeping those hands high. You've seen I'm a decent shot, and that I have no compunction about killing a man, so unless you want to breathe your last in this here pass, you'll do exactly as I say.'

Leach dismounted then raised his hands, but only so that they were at shoulder-level. Ethan appraised his stance, then glanced at Amelia.

'You reckon you can hold a gun on him while I search him?'

'I will do no such thing when you haven't explained yourself.'

'Ma'am, believe me, I just ain't got the time to explain what I'm doing, but I *do* need you to hold this gun on him.'

Amelia sighed, then nodded. After Ethan and she had dismounted, she walked towards him, holding out a hand, but Ethan stood behind her and placed the gun in her hands. He chivvied her hands up until the gun was sighting Leach's chest, then stood to her side.

'If he does anything untoward, shoot him.'

Then Ethan paced around Leach. From behind, he slipped Leach's gun from its holster and hurled it away, then frisked him. Throughout his ministrations Leach stared aloft, but then twitched when Ethan found the concealed knife in his boot. Ethan knelt then moved to slide the knife out, but Leach took the opportunity to kick him.

Ethan had anticipated this move and grabbed Leach's leg, then yanked the knife out, but Leach dug his heel in the ground, pivoted on the leg, and tried to knock Ethan over with his other leg.

Ethan merely danced back, letting Amelia have a clear shot at Leach, but when he glanced at her, she was shaking and the gun barrel was travelling in small circles.

Leach laughed then hurled himself at Ethan, but Ethan leapt to the side, letting Leach fall to the ground and land flat on his belly. As Leach shook off his fall, Ethan dashed towards Amelia, aiming to reclaim his gun, but Leach lunged and grabbed a trailing foot, holding on even as Ethan dragged him across the ground.

Ethan kicked out, aiming to shake Leach off, but the blow only loosened his own footing and he slipped to his knees. Leach climbed his hands up Ethan's legs then launched himself at him, slamming him to the ground. As he fell, Ethan twisted, but he only managed a half-turn and was just able to throw up an arm and loop it around Leach's neck.

He wrestled him down, but Leach used his small amount of leverage to punch Ethan in the kidneys, then a second time. This loosened Ethan's grasp and he fell back. In a moment, Leach was on him, his hands at his throat.

But then Leach's eyes opened wide. A pained screech ripped from his mouth as he tumbled away. Ethan had embedded his own knife in his chest. Leach rolled over to lie on his back, the knife hilt pointing skywards.

As Amelia shrieked her shock, Leach hurled his hands to the knife. He gave a slight tug, but then his reddened hands fell away. He twitched once, then was still.

Ethan grabbed his shoulders and dragged him to the side of the trail, then went to Amelia's side and held out a hand, palm up.

'The gun, now,' he said.

'You . . . You . . . You killed him.'

'I sure did.'

'I . . . I have nothing to steal.' She firmed her shoulders, then turned the gun on him, all the time backing away. 'But if you try anything with me, I will kill you.'

'I don't doubt it. But you won't get trouble from me. Just give me the gun, then get on your horse and keep on riding.'

'I am not trusting you,' she murmured, backing away another pace.

Ethan advanced on her. 'If you want to live long enough to wed that sweetheart of yours, you'll do exactly as I say. Now, move!'

With a last glance at Leach, Amelia slapped the gun into Ethan's hand, then stomped to her horse. She mounted it, then without looking at Ethan, headed for the end of the pass at a fair trot.

Ethan mounted his own horse and hurried after her to draw alongside.

'You don't need to follow me,' she said. 'I'll complete the rest of the journey on my own. And I can ride faster than this.'

'I'm sure you can, but this is just the right speed.' Ethan pointed to the end of the pass, now one hundred yards ahead. 'But when we emerge from the pass, you'll slow down to our former pace.'

Amelia jutted her jaw, but then swung her head to the side.

'I am not listening to a murderer.'

'You hired me after I killed that rancher.'

'Then, you were saving another person's life, but however disagreeable Mr Oldrich was, he was no threat to either of us.'

'He was, and you got to trust me on this. Slow, now!'

Amelia still rode on at the same pace, then, with a tug on the reins, slowed her horse as they emerged

26

from the pass.

'I've slowed.' She glanced at him. 'Now you have one minute to explain yourself before I leave you.'

'I will, but while I'm talking, don't look at me too much and don't look towards the butte beside us.'

'The butte?' She glanced to her side, but then, with a snap of her neck, faced the front. 'Why should I not look at the butte?'

'Just keep your head forward, but from the corner of your eye, look out and all will become clear.'

For 200 yards or so they rode on at a steady pace, but just as Amelia started to rock her head from side to side in irritation, Ethan saw it again. And Amelia straightened, too.

'I saw a flash,' she said.

'Yeah. Somebody is signalling.'

'Signalling what?'

'No idea, but I don't reckon he has our best interests in mind.'

'I understand, but that was no reason to kill Mr Oldrich.'

'It was every reason. He's taken you on the most circuitous and most dangerous route to White Creek he could find. And he was just being too insistent that we went through a gorge when somebody is signalling nearby.'

'After two days in that man's company, I am not surprised that he was engaged in a nefarious scheme, but I have no money to steal.'

'Perhaps you don't, but I guess your family is rich?'

'You could say that.' Amelia raised her chin. 'And I am in your hands. What should I do?'

'Continue to ride at the same pace. Every mile we get closer to Bear Pass is another mile we won't have to cover at speed. But that signaller is wondering what's happened to Leach. Before long, he'll investigate and that ambush will come. So, when I give the signal, ride like your life depends on it – because it does.'

Amelia nodded and they rode on.

From the corner of his eye, Ethan saw more flashes. One came from someone towards the top of the butte. The other came from further down the slope, and although he couldn't see either person, the flashes were both moving to lower ground.

With a sideways glance at Amelia, Ethan hurried his horse to a faster trot, but not enough to be obvious.

From what he'd heard about Bear Pass, he judged that at this pace it was a good half-hour away along a stony but level rough trail.

Ahead, the long arc of the River Green was slowly revealing itself to them. But from the swollen and brown water, and the faint roaring that he could hear, Ethan judged that they wouldn't find a passing place other than at the ferry at Bear Pass.

Then another flash came, this time just 200 yards to his side and, for the first time, he saw movement as someone slipped behind a rock.

Ethan maintained his steady pace, although he did look at Amelia until she looked at him, then provided an encouraging smile. But as he turned back, he saw movement again as someone disappeared behind a short tangle of boulders, just one hundred yards to the side and slightly ahead of him.

'We're going for it any moment now,' he said.

'Just give the word, Mr Craig.'

Ethan kept his gaze set forward, but ensured he watched the boulders, waiting for the moment when someone should emerge from behind them. Between them and the boulders, there was just flat land.

Then a rider appeared, nudging his horse forward.

'Now,' Ethan said.

He immediately kicked his horse into full speed. Amelia followed him a moment later, but Ethan didn't wait to check that she was riding as fast as she could; he concentrated on getting past the boulders and gaining as much distance as he could before the ambushers organized themselves.

For a full minute he rode on, then glanced back. Amelia was two horse lengths behind him, but 300 yards behind her a straggling line of riders were now pursuing. Ethan counted three men, but just as a burst of confidence hit him, a group of riders emerged from higher up the butte, and then another group emerged at their side. These groups were a half-mile away, but they were heading on an angle towards them and aiming to head them off further down the trail.

'How far to Bear Pass?' Amelia shouted.

'At this speed, not long, but our horses ain't going to keep up the pace, and either way, I reckon I'll need to take a few of them out.'

'In the circumstances I have no problem with that.'

Ethan glanced at the bulky bags behind Amelia, which were jostling up and down as she rode.

'Drop those bags and lighten your load, or I'll have to kill the whole lot of them to get you to Bear Pass.'

'I *do* have a problem with that. All my clothes are—'

'And what's more important, your life or your clothes?'

Amelia peered at him with a stern-jawed expression that suggested she had to think about this, then shivered and leaned back to unhook two bags.

For his part, Ethan unhooked the bag containing his spare clothes and cooking-pans, but as they rattled to the ground behind him, he saw that Amelia had not unhooked the largest bag.

As he dropped back to flank her, he glared hard at the bag, but she shook her head.

'That may be large,' she said, 'but it isn't heavy.'

'Let it go.'

'It contains my wedding-dress, and all this effort will be worthless unless I have a dress to get wed in.'

Ethan considered swinging from the saddle to swipe the bag away, but judged that she was probably right and one dress wouldn't be that heavy.

He nodded, but then the following riders fired their first shot at them. It was high and possibly intended as a warning shot, but this just encouraged Ethan to head on.

They rounded a rocky outcrop, reaching it ahead of the men who were aiming to outflank them, then swung round to join the trail from Tarrat's Gorge and on down towards Bear Pass beyond. The small settlement that nestled on this side of the river was now just four miles ahead. But with their straining horses slowing with every pace, Ethan reckoned that that distance would feel like it was twice as long.

He glanced over his shoulder to see the riders had now clumped as they swung round the outcrop and, as barked orders drifted to Ethan, they drew their guns. They all fired skywards. Ethan again ignored them and, as one, the men swung their guns down and started firing at them.

They were still too far away to get in any accurate shooting, but with the sustained fire, someone just had to get lucky before long.

Ethan urged Amelia to hurry on ahead, then fell back. He slotted in behind her, then laid down a quick burst of gunfire over his shoulder. His fifth shot wheeled one man from his horse and this encouraged the other riders to slow.

As Ethan reloaded, Amelia had already gained fifty yards on him and he gained the additional advantage that the riders stayed the same distance back from him as they had before.

Ethan glanced forward, seeing that the settlement was now just three miles ahead, then fired back again. This time, all his shots were wild, and the men became bolder, hurrying on and splitting, aiming to come at him from both sides of the trail.

Ethan reloaded, but saved his shots until they made their move, contented that every galloped pace before they moved was another pace closer to Bear Pass.

Then they came, swooping in from both sides and

hollering like banshees.

Ethan alternated firing left and right, winging one man in the shoulder, then hammering another man to the ground. But still they came, hurtling in towards him.

Lead whistled past his head and past his chest, the blows close enough for him to imagine they had scythed through his body. Ethan gritted his teeth and spurred his horse, seeking a burst of speed that would either kill his steed or get him to the settlement, now under two miles ahead.

With repeated lead clattering behind him, he closed on Amelia, then hurried on to draw alongside her.

She flashed him a pained glance that said she thought they wouldn't make it, too, but Ethan mustered an encouraging yell, then pointed ahead at the settlement. He could now see the ferry and make out the forms of men who were heading to their horses in response to the gunfire.

'Help's on the way,' Ethan shouted. 'We just got to keep going.'

Ethan spurred his horse, now seeing the riders in Bear Pass galloping towards them, but they were still over a mile away from safety.

Then Amelia shrieked. Ethan looked to the side, thinking for one terrible moment that she'd been hit, but she was slowing as she peered at the riders.

'What you doing?' Ethan shouted.

'It's . . .' She shrieked again and Ethan saw a streak of red explode from her horse's right flank. The horse's rear leg buckled and it stumbled, then went to its knees, the jerking movement throwing Amelia over its head. As the beast flopped on its side, she hit the ground and rolled, coming to a shuddering halt.

Ethan dragged his horse to a halt and circled back to join her as the ambushers bore down on them.

Amelia rolled to her feet, swayed, then limped towards her horse. Ethan thought she was on a futile mission to get it to rise, but then saw her grab the bag containing her wedding-dress, then swing round to face Ethan and raise a hand.

Ethan pulled his horse to a halt beside her and thrust out a hand to help her on to the back of his steed, but by now the riders were all within thirty yards and spreading out to surround him. Ethan quickly judged that two people on his tiring horse wouldn't get another hundred yards before the men cut them off.

He jumped down from his horse, grabbed Amelia's hand, and dragged her to her wounded horse, then pushed her down to lie between its quivering legs. She flinched away, but a shot gouged into the dirt by her feet and she thrust her head down. Ethan joined her and hunkered down then, using the horse as a shield, concentrated on taking careful aim and dispatching as many men as he could.

He blasted two men from their mounts as they approached, but then the riders laid down a sustained burst of gunfire. Ethan had no choice but to thrust his head down and, with Amelia, search for every scrap of cover he could find.

The sickening thud of lead gouging into flesh

surrounded them as the horse received repeated blows. But Ethan ignored the men coming at him from the other side of the horse and looked in the opposite direction, waiting for the first man to seek a direct view of him.

Then two riders surged in. Ethan hammered lead into the first, but the second swung down from his horse and Ethan heard his feet pounding as he charged round to get closer to them. Beside him, Amelia cringed down seeking to burrow herself beneath the horse's stomach.

Then the man appeared, zigzagging towards the horse, with two other men following him. Ethan raised his gun to fire at the nearest, but then that man stumbled forwards. He ran on for another two paces, then fell to his knees and keeled over on to his front, a flurry of gunsmoke rising from his back.

The other two men skidded to a halt, then fired over their shoulders.

Ethan whooped, realizing that the men from Bear Pass had arrived. He risked glancing up to see a row of seven men heading towards them, then over his shoulder to see that the ambushers, now more than a dozen, were falling back.

He patted Amelia's arm and, when their saviours hurtled on to join them, ventured out to confirm that the attacking men had now pulled back. So, he grabbed Amelia's arm and slipped out from the horse. Keeping low, they hurried to Ethan's steed.

Ethan gave everyone a quick acknowledgement, then swung Amelia up behind him and, with the men flanking them on all sides, hurried down to Bear Pass.

'Got to thank you,' Ethan shouted.

'No trouble,' the lead man shouted. 'We reckoned we'd freed Bear Pass of those sorts.'

'There's always more of that kind around.'

With the pursuing men staying well back, they rode on down into the settlement. Ethan glanced back frequently, but the pursuers kept out of firing range, and when they swung round to ride down the main road that approached the ferry, these men pulled to a halt and watched their progress.

The rescuers helped them down from their horse and, without formality, directed them to the ferry.

'Don't worry,' the lead man said, slapping his holster, 'they ain't getting past us to cross our river.'

Ethan nodded. 'I don't doubt it.'

Ethan led his horse on to the ferry, with Amelia carrying her wedding-dress bag over her shoulder, then leaned on the rail at the front.

The men gestured across the river and the winch-handlers on the other side encouraged their oxen to trudge in a circle and wind the winch that would drag the ferry across the river.

With a lurch, the ferry set off. Ethan watched the riverside recede slowly, then lifted his gaze to see the ambushers who had massed on the edge of town. Their numbers were reduced, but there were still around a dozen men, and even with only seven men in the settlement facing them, Ethan reckoned they could hold them off.

But then, from higher up the trail, he saw another group of at least twelve riders appear.

And the men on the outskirts of Bear Pass were waving them on.

CHAPTER 4

A quarter of the way across the river, Ethan could only watch the battle lines form in Bear Pass. The small band of defenders had their backs to the river while, down the road, the other men massed.

The attackers took up positions behind every available scrap of cover: barrels, hollows in the road, around the sides of the buildings. Within seconds, they were peppering gunfire at the small band of defenders. But these men fought back with the resolute determination of men used to defending their livelihood.

Foot by foot, Ethan and Amelia drew away from the riverside, but on land, foot by foot, the attackers were closing in on the defenders. First, they winged one man into the water. Then they dropped another man, and all the time they advanced, searching for cover nearer and nearer to the water.

They winged another man and forced a division in the ranks when two men jumped up and ran down the riverside. At first Ethan thought they were trying to outflank the attackers, but then saw they were running to preserve their lives. And as that left just two men, with one of them being wounded, it was just moments before the raiders overwhelmed them and reached the water.

The ferry was now at the mid-point of the river, the turbulent water swaying it back and forth. On the other side of the river, the winch-handlers were ignoring the oxen as they stared at the disaster that had taken place on the other side.

'Surely those men can't force their way across the river, can they?' Amelia asked.

'I don't see how they can make anyone drag them across. They'll just have to find another way, and I don't think that'll be easy. We should get some distance on them before they can come after us.'

'But can't they pull the ferry back?'

Ethan considered the arrangement of ropes and judged that they could stop the trailing rope from playing out if they could find a way to secure it, which would strand them in the centre of the river. But that would also create an impasse that wouldn't help any of them.

'No,' he said. 'They ain't going to kidnap you.'

'If you say so,' Amelia murmured, her voice wavering for the first time.

Ethan glanced back at her to see that her eyes were downcast as she fingered her sole remaining bag with shaking hands.

'Don't worry,' he said and stared at her until she looked up and flashed a wan smile. 'But are you going to tell me why you slowed down on the trail?'

Amelia gulped. 'I recognized the man leading

those raiders, a Mr Buck Lincoln. He used to work for my father.'

'He got any grievance against your family?'

'Not that I know of.'

'But you must . . .'

The ferry lurched, throwing Ethan into the rail. He righted himself, but then the ferry snapped round and he had to clutch the rail to avoid being tumbled into the water.

He hung on, bent double and staring down at the milling water, then pushed himself straight and walked his way down the rail to Amelia's side. He grabbed her arm, but she ignored his offers of help and pointed over Ethan's shoulder.

Ethan looked back to see that Buck Lincoln's raiders had commandeered the winch on their side of the river but instead of trying to drag them back, they'd cut the rope. Now, the coils were playing out into the water and trailing downstream.

With no guidance to keep them on a straight course, the rope connecting hem to the other side of the river was anchoring them in place and forcing them to arc around. At a healthy rate, they were heading downstream and swinging towards a point fifty yards down the river bank.

Ethan and Amelia hung on with their backs to the rail as the vessel scythed through the water. Every choppy swell rocked the ferry, but it was wide and Ethan judged that it was solid enough to avoid capsizing.

But then a wild lurch and grinding of timbers threw him to the bottom of the ferry. He skidded across the timbers, Amelia at his side also sliding onwards.

The lowest rail was three feet off the ground and he was heading at speed towards it on his back. But he pushed up both legs, planting them firmly on the rail, and halted his plunge towards the river.

The rail creaked, splinters flying, but it held, letting him throw out a hand and grab Amelia's arm, halting her slide, but her extra weight dragged a huge creak from the rail and then a crack. With Amelia's arm held firmly, Ethan threw himself to the side. He rolled away as the rail broke and entangled, they tumbled to a halt with Ethan's feet dangling in the water.

He looked up to see that the ferry was still turning, but then it lurched to a halt again, throwing them to the other side of the vessel. Ethan swung round, and again raised his feet to stop them from tumbling into the water, but this time, the lurch wasn't as strong as before and the rail held.

He rolled to his knees and searched for what had happened, then saw that the rope connecting them to the other side of the river had snagged on a protruding boulder. That had stopped their arcing progress. And now they were trapped, the force of the water heading downstream mooring them on the boulder.

The men in Bear Pass were shouting, but he couldn't hear what they were saying. He reckoned they were probably working out whether they could drag them past the boulder, or whether playing out more rope might shift them more readily.

But one thing was certain: the downstream force was swinging the ferry from side to side and, from the grinding of the timbers beneath his feet, there were other rocks beneath the ferry and it would break up before the men could free them. And, on the other side of the river, Buck Lincoln's men had grouped and were laying down systematic gunfire at them. From such a distance, the shots plumed into the water, but they were getting closer and before long, somebody would sight them.

Another huge creak issued from below, again throwing Ethan to the bottom of the ferry. He glanced at Amelia to see that she had looped an arm around the bottom rail and was hanging on. Her other arm clutched the bag containing her wedding-dress. His horse was kicking and was spooked enough to break free and dive into the river.

He had no choice. He pulled Leach's knife from his boot and crawled to the back of the ferry. He placed the knife to the rope that secured them to the riverside. He glanced at Amelia, receiving a short nod, then sliced down.

He sawed, the wet rope at first resisting his attempts, but once he had teased the strands apart, they frayed, then ripped apart, the tension in them aiding their demise. Before the last strand snapped, Ethan rolled back to avoid the whiplash, then looped his arm around the rail on the opposite side of the ferry to Amelia.

Then the rope snapped and, with surprising grace, the ferry moved off. It had already aligned itself with the flow of the water and they glided serenely away.

Ethan looked back to see Buck Lincoln's men try one last flurry of shots, but they all fell short. Then he glanced at the men in Bear Pass, who were gesturing at him. From their frantic waves they were clearly delivering a warning, but about what Ethan couldn't tell.

'You fine?' he shouted over the roaring of the river.

'Yes,' Amelia shouted, 'but when you cut that rope, did you consider how you'd steer us?'

'I always worry about one problem at a time.' Ethan glanced at the moiling brown river at his side. 'But I reckon this river is stronger than I am and it'll decide where we're going.'

'What's ahead?'

He craned his neck to look forward, seeing that for the next half-mile the banks on both sides of the river were precipitous. Beyond that, he couldn't see.

'Got no idea. I've never been downriver.'

Ethan avoided mentioning that as Bear Pass had sprung up at the easiest place to cross the river, he didn't hold out much hope that the strength of the river would lessen for many miles. But he consoled himself with the thought that they were travelling in the right direction at a good speed, and it would be hard for Buck Lincoln to get close enough to deliver pot-shots at them.

'But still,' she shouted, 'it would be wise to get to the side, and I believe you don't have to beat the river to get there. You just have to steer the ferry with a rudder.'

Ethan tried to convey that he'd already thought of

that with a knowing nod, then shuffled to the broken rail. He worked it from side to side until it came loose, then crawled to the back of the ferry. There, he again looped an arm around the bottom rail and stuck the rail in the water, but angled away from the riverside.

He kept his gaze set forward, trying to judge whether this was helping, but was unable to tell whether he was directing them any closer. But he reckoned it at least gave him a chance of steering if more boulders appeared ahead.

Amelia also stared ahead, watching the water and, from her frequent glances between the riverside and the route ahead, Ethan reckoned she was growing increasingly worried.

'At least you still have your wedding-dress,' he shouted.

She clutched her bag to her chest. 'At least that.'

'And you got one hell of a story to tell your sweet-heart.'

'I believe he may be impressed with this exploit. But that doesn't stop me wishing it hadn't happened.'

'Me, too. You thought of any reason why Buck Lincoln is after you?'

'I can think of no grievance that would make him want to kidnap me.'

'It's worse than that. He cut the rope, and that means he doesn't want to take you alive.'

Amelia sighed. 'I believe you're right.'

Ethan watched her turn to peer ahead. He waited, having detected a change in her tone when he'd suggested that Buck's motives were murderous, but when she didn't turn back, he coughed.

'Amelia,' he said, 'I reckon you have an idea what this is about and you're thinking about it. But I also reckon that however much learning you got at Mrs Haversham's school for young ladies, it didn't teach you how to understand men like Buck Lincoln. I know his type. So, just tell me what you're thinking and I'll . . . we'll figure it out.'

Amelia shuffled round to look at Ethan.

'I don't know why Mr Lincoln would want to kill me. But it is possible he wants to stop me being wed.'

'Why?'

'When my father died, his will stated that his ranch would only pass on to his descendant if that descendant was married before reaching the age of twenty-one.'

'That's an odd thing to put on his kin.'

'He devised it for my brother's sake. He was wild and reckless without a . . . Well, it doesn't matter now. My father intended the will to force him to rein in his exuberance. And it did. He calmed and was all set to wed, but then he died in a fire at the family home, and that meant I would inherit the ranch.'

'And that clause still stands?'

'Yes.' She fingered the bag. 'It was intended for my brother, but it binds me as well. And I must wed before I am twenty-one, or I will not inherit.'

'And when are you twenty-one?'

'On Friday, my wedding-day.'

'And who will inherit if you don't marry by then?'

'My uncle.' Amelia looked over her shoulder to

face the river ahead. 'But he's been looking after the ranch while I've been away, and he isn't behind this.'

'I can understand why you got faith in your kin, but men do terrible things for money.'

'I know that.' She turned and smiled. 'But I am marrying his son.'

Ethan raised his eyebrows. 'And that would be your cousin?'

'No. My uncle isn't real kin. He was just my father's best friend and, to me, he will always be my uncle.' Amelia frowned. 'But whether I marry Wesley or not, Wesley's family will have a stake in my father's ranch.'

'Then I guess the mystery stands. Someone must gain by stopping you marrying Wesley, and when you figure out who that is, you'll know why Buck is after you.' Ethan smiled. 'But either way, it won't work. Because you will get wed if it's the last thing I do.'

Amelia beamed a real smile. 'I don't doubt you will succeed, Mr Craig.'

'And, Amelia, please start calling me Ethan sometime before we get to White Creek.'

'I will do that, Mr Cr ... Ethan.' She shuffled round to look along the sheer banks of the river. 'And if I am to get to White Creek, it'd help to get off this river. Are we getting any closer to the side?'

Ethan looked to the side, judging that if anything they had veered even further away.

'A little.'

He considered the small rudder he had, then glanced around the ferry looking for other ways to steer it. But, on seeing nothing, he stared at the water, trying to understand the seething currents and how he could use them.

But in the time since they had left Bear Pass, the river had gained in ferocity and the roaring that had now become their constant companion had grown, too. And ahead, the noise was even fiercer.

Ethan narrowed his eyes as he stared ahead. The noise suggested to him that they were approaching a length of rapids, and as he didn't fancy their chances of surviving a journey through them, he reckoned he had to get to the side as soon as possible.

Ethan thrust the rudder first one way, then the other, searching for what would work best in steering the ferry, but his efforts gave no apparent benefit and he decided that the rail was too short and thin.

He withdrew it, rolled to his knees, then his feet, and searched for the easiest rail to dislodge. But as he shuffled round the ferry, the noise from ahead grew again. An insistent rumbling filled the air, and the temperature was dropping. Ethan looked ahead, seeing a rising patch of fog.

Ethan had never seen rapids on a river this large, and couldn't see why they would force such volumes of water into the air.

Then he saw what at first appeared to be a line across the river: a solid block where the brown mass ended and a lighter swirling mass started.

Then he realized that the line wasn't a change in the colour of the water.

'Waterfall,' he murmured.

CHAPTER 5

'What do we do?' Amelia shouted.

'We got to get to the side,' Ethan shouted over the roar of the approaching waterfall. 'Find something to paddle with.'

'Like what?'

Ethan jumped to the side of the ferry and slammed his rail into the water, then swirled it back and forth, but the wood just scythed through the water with no effect.

'I don't know. Hands, feet, anything you got.'

Amelia crawled to the side and scooped a handful of water away, then looked up.

'That isn't enough.'

'I know! But have you got a better idea?'

'You need resistance to your strokes.' She slapped the bottom of the ferry. 'What about one of these planks?'

'That'll sink the ferry.'

Amelia looked at him with her eyebrows raised in an expression that said that sinking was the least of their worries.

Ethan nodded, then thrust the rail beneath a gap in the planks.

He prised out the end of a plank, revealing the milling river below, then walked it up into the air, peeling it away with a desperate series of creaks that shuddered the whole ferry.

With one last tug, he dragged the plank loose and carried it to the side of the ferry where he rowed using furious deep strokes that splashed water all around him. But the ferry was rapidly building up pace, and he didn't detect any sideways movement from his actions.

He broke off another plank and passed it to Amelia. She sat beside him and paddled, but they only turned the ferry a mite and they weren't getting any closer to the side.

And the waterfall was getting closer and closer. The roaring was deafening, the end of the river, which might as well be the end of the world, now just one hundred yards ahead.

Ethan paddled with frantic strokes and he saw that they were now steering a course at an angle to the waterfall. And he judged that if they were really lucky, they'd go over the waterfall only fifty yards from the riverside and not the sixty they'd get on a straight course.

With a hopeless hollow in his guts, he continued to paddle. Around him, he saw more of the detritus flowing down the river. Logs and bushes swirled along, and he couldn't help but follow their progress as they headed to the end, then slipped over the side.

One log carried on, sticking five yards over the

side before tumbling away, and in it, Ethan saw their fate, now just seconds away.

He stopped paddling and hurled the plank away, then staggered to his feet and shuffled to the front of the ferry.

He unhitched his horse, then raised his hand to encourage it to bolt. The frightened animal needed no encouragement to tear itself away, then plough through the rail and dive into the water. It bobbed up, but then swirled away towards the edge, now just twenty-five yards ahead.

'You let it go,' Amelia shouted.

'I had to give it a chance. And that's our only chance, too. We got to get clear of the ferry.'

Amelia glanced ahead, then nodded. She grabbed her bag, then held out a hand for Ethan to help her up. Then they slipped under the rail to stand on the side of the ferry and, on the count of three, leapt in the water.

The cold hit Ethan, dragging a deep breath from him that was as much water as air. He was aware he'd released Amelia's hand as he'd hit, and he searched around for her. But the pounding water filled his eyes and ears, and he couldn't even work out which way was up to fight his way to the surface.

But then he realized he'd lost all weight and he was falling through the open air. He just had time to see that a wall of water was rushing up to meet him before he closed his eyes and gritted his teeth for the impact.

'You fine?' Ethan asked.

Amelia opened her eyes and peered around, looking at the roaring fire, then down at the horse blanket that he'd wrapped her in.

'I am, but . . .' She glanced at Ethan, who was sitting in his underclothes, then at the drying line of both their clothes that he'd strung up beside the fire. She gulped. 'Why am I . . . What am I . . .'

'Relax. We're safe.' Ethan patted her arm, then rolled back on his haunches. 'We went over the waterfall and the force of hitting the water knocked you unconscious. I managed to stay conscious and found you, then got you to the side. But we lost everything.'

Ethan cupped his ear, then pointed back through the trees. In the gaps between the trunks, the view was white from the water droplets around the waterfall, but as they were a few hundred yards from the water, the noise was only a low rumbling.

'I am most obliged to you for dragging me to safety.' She rustled under the blanket, then took a deep breath and lifted the blanket an inch to peer beneath.

'Quit worrying,' Ethan murmured. 'I had to undress you to dry your clothes, but you ain't got anything I ain't seen before.' Ethan pointed at her clothes drying beside the fire. 'And I've let you stew in your under . . . your underthings.'

'I am obliged for that, but I am still damp.' She peered at him, but when Ethan just looked back, she twirled a finger indicating that he should turn around.

Ethan shrugged but turned and faced the fire. He

heard her rustling as she struggled under the blanket. Then she padded by him with the blanket gripped tightly under her chin and holding a handful of garments which Ethan avoided looking at with a determined swing of his head.

But when she returned from hanging them on spare twigs around the fire, he smiled.

'You hungry?' he asked.

Amelia smiled for the first time since coming to.

'I am.'

'Me, too.'

Amelia snorted. 'You not catch anything?'

'I guess you think I'm the kind of man who'll head into the forest and catch all manner of animals, cook them up with some wild herbs and leaves, then fashion a boat out of sticks.'

'I'd hoped you might.'

'Then you're wrong. You picked the wrong man to escort you to White Creek. I ain't much use as a frontiersman man. Now, give me a poker-table and I'll show you something.'

'You have already proved you are resourceful in your own way.' She fingered her scalp, wincing when her questing fingers brushed a sore spot. 'But this still leaves me with a problem.'

'I know, but as soon as you're dry and we're rested up, we'll be on our way.' Ethan glanced skywards. 'Although that might be tomorrow. It's getting too late to travel.'

'I didn't mean that. Now, there's no point getting me to White Creek on time.' She raised her chin and blinked back a tear. 'I've lost everything.'

Ethan furrowed his brow, then nodded. 'You mean your wedding-dress?'

'Yes.'

'You got your life. I guess your sweetheart would be more concerned with that than some dress.'

'He might, but I am not. I have spent months in sewing-class making that dress and I have dreamed of being wed in it.' She shuffled her knees up to her chest and clutched them, then rocked back and forth. 'And now, I won't.'

Ethan stared at her until she looked up, tears welling, then winked and slipped into the bushes. He returned with a bulky and folded dress.

'Then it's a good job I jumped back in the river and rescued this here dress for you, ain't it?'

'You saved it!' Amelia blurted out as Ethan held up her dress.

'I couldn't save the bonnet, mind.'

'The bonnet doesn't matter. I can get another one.'

Ethan placed the dress in her lap. 'And it got all tangled up in a tree and got ripped.'

'I can mend it.'

She threw her arms around his neck and hugged him, then sat back, smiling as she parted the folds of wet material to reveal a jagged and dirty tear.

'And you're welcome.' Ethan coughed and pointed. 'But watch out for your blanket. It's slipped and I can see the tops of your—'

'Mr Craig,' she murmured, gathering up her blanket and edging back to the side of the fire. 'You are a most incor . . . What was that?'

'What was what?'

Amelia peered into the darkening forest with her eyes narrowed. 'That noise, like a grunt.'

'Like a grunt, eh? Well, I reckon that was an animal.'

'What kind of animal?'

'Probably a bear.' Ethan raised his eyebrows and lowered his voice. 'Or perhaps something even worse.'

She gulped. 'What's even worse than a bear?'

Ethan watched her eyes open wide, then chuckled. 'For a woman who got schooled at Mrs Haversham's school for young ladies, you're awful easy to jest.'

'Mr Craig, you will stop finding everything about this appalling situation amusing and find out what is out there.'

Ethan nodded and rolled to his feet. With his gun drawn, he headed to the edge of their camp-fire and peered into the gathering darkness. Behind him, he heard Amelia padding closer, but he gestured at her to stay back, then stood with his ear cocked high.

A rustling sounded deep in the darkness. Then night birds called to each other in a manner that to Ethan sounded real, and so it wasn't a man signalling to another man. He turned, but at that moment, a hawk screeched into the air and flapped through the undergrowth to gain its freedom.

Amelia screamed as she slapped her hands over her ears.

'What was that?' she cried, peering up and around.

'Just some bird, and nothing to worry about.'

She took a deep breath as Ethan joined her.

'I suppose you're going to tell me to not be so jumpy.'

'I am telling you that. But I'm also telling you more one thing.' Ethan looked her up and down and gave a low whistle. 'You've dropped your blanket.'

CHAPTER 6

At sun-up, Ethan headed down to the river and watched the sun rise to get his bearings.

Before Buck's men had attacked, their planned route was to head from Bear Pass to Green Valley where they'd pick up the train for White Creek on Thursday.

Although he hadn't been this way before, he presumed that the trail from Bear Pass to his left and Green Valley to his right must cross somewhere ahead. And that meant they'd have to leave the river to reach it.

Keeping his bearings by following the river would be easier and, as it swung round to be just a dozen or so miles south of Green Valley, it might be a more prudent journey. But he judged that getting out of the thick forest and on to that trail would cover more distance with greater speed.

So, he headed back to the camp. Amelia was waiting for him and they headed north, keeping the river at their backs and the sun to their right.

They walked through the morning, the rising sun

rippling through the tree trunks as it rose until it warmed their backs, but matted vegetation coated the ground and every pace was hard-fought. They had no choice but to follow animal tracks that led them on routes that veered wildly off their chosen direction. And it was long hours before the sound of the rushing river behind them faded into the background.

Ethan led and was pleased that he never had to wait for Amelia to catch up with him. When he'd first met her, he'd judged her a prim and probably spoilt woman, but from her courage in the face of danger and her fortitude after disaster, he now started to view her as the resilient daughter of a rancher.

But he still dreaded hearing the question he expected her to ask. The sun was at its highest when at last he finally heard it.

'Mr Craig,' she said, 'do you know where we're going?'

Ethan pointed ahead. 'That-a-way.'

She stopped and set a hand on a hip. 'In other words, we're lost.'

'Nope. We're just heading on until we reach the trail.'

'And how far is that?'

'Just a little way now.'

'It was just a little way when we set off this morning.'

Ethan paced to a halt and turned to face her.

'And have you got a better idea?'

'I believe travelling on the lower ground is wrong.' Amelia gestured to the ground, then pointed up. 'We should head for the nearest slope.'

'If we go uphill, we got to go down again. It's better to stay down.'

'If we go up, we might get a view of the surrounding area. And we wouldn't have to stay lost.'

'We are not lost,' Ethan intoned through gritted teeth.

'Then what are we?'

'We are . . . we are looking for the trail.'

Amelia stared at him, but when his irritation at her criticism had receded and he relaxed his stance, she smiled.

'And?'

'And perhaps,' he murmured, 'we should head to higher ground where we might see further.'

Ethan beckoned ahead, letting Amelia lead. She looked around, then continued on the same path as before. But a half-mile on, they reached a grouping of animal tracks and she followed the ones that headed uphill.

Ethan glanced at the sun, judging that this route was veering off towards the west, but he kept quiet. And then had to bite his lip when the track swung round to head due north.

They rose steadily and the trees thinned, but they still didn't gain a view of the surrounding area. It took almost an hour before they felt like they'd crested a hill, the undergrowth being so thick they couldn't tell whether there was more hill ahead to climb.

And it was only when the general direction of the ground was downwards that they felt sure they'd crested it. Ethan didn't offer an opinion, now only annoyed that Amelia's good idea hadn't worked out, but then ahead, he detected a lightening in the tangle of trees. He didn't mention this, but within another fifty yards, Amelia was looking back at him and Ethan couldn't help but return a smile.

They speeded. Ethan didn't expect that they'd reached the trail, and they hadn't, but they had found an area where the wind had toppled several trees and they, in turn, had brought down the surrounding trees. And over the canopy they could see the surrounding area.

But all they could see was forest, followed by more forest.

Ethan paced around the cleared area, and at the far side, he could see back along the route they'd taken. And the river was depressingly close. He could believe that he just had to reach out to touch it, but they had taken almost two-thirds of the day to reach this spot.

He traced back along the length of the river. He couldn't see the waterfall, but he could see the tree-less area and the gorge around which Buck had chased them. He could therefore see where Bear Pass was, but aside from that, he could see only trees.

'Amelia,' he said, 'I reckon you have to make a decision. We can see where Bear Pass is and I reckon we can reach there if we head on a straight line towards the setting sun. We probably won't get there tonight, but we will get there.'

'Or we carry on being lost?'

'We aren't lost. We can see where we are.'

'But we don't know where the trail to Green Valley is.'

Ethan sighed. 'I guess we don't. We can carry on looking, and we might find it. And if we meet some-one heading in the same way, we can still get to Green Valley in time for the train.'

'But heading to Bear Pass probably means I'll miss it?'

'Yeah. On the other hand, Buck Lincoln will find a way across that river soon and then Bear Pass will be safer than the open trail.'

Amelia stared towards Bear Pass, then swung round to peer at the forest.

'I choose to remain lost.'

'Then we'll do that.' Ethan stared at the lay of the land. 'And if the trail swings east, I reckon it'll take a route along the lowest land.'

He pointed to a valley that swung round to pass by them. Amelia agreed to their new direction and they headed off. But his flash of optimism at finding a possible place where the trail could be eroded quickly as they made painfully slow progress down the hill.

Long before Ethan judged that they'd reached the valley, the light level dropped and he became increasingly aware of his grumbling stomach and the fact that his chances of catching anything to eat were remote.

But just as he was looking for a place to camp, through the trees he saw a lighter slash arcing round to the west. Whether this was the trail or a river, he didn't know, but he trudged on towards it, even getting ahead of Amelia in his haste. Then he slid to a halt.

Amelia was tramping her feet and watching them to avoid tripping and so toppled into his back, then hung on to his shoulders.

'Why have you stopped?'

Ethan pointed. Ahead lay a well-travelled trail rutted with thick wagon-tracks.

'The trail,' he said, weary pride in his voice. 'And it only took us a whole day to find it.'

'And we're only a whole day behind schedule.'

Ethan made a fire and, when the flames had taken hold, sat in the widest clearing he could find. Staying quiet, he searched for birds or animals to take a pot-shot at, but despite hearing many sounds around him, the wildlife saw him before he saw them.

He returned to report his lack of progress to Amelia, but she was standing by the fire and looking down towards the trail. Ethan turned to see that a wagon laden with bulging bags had pulled up and the owner was staring up at them.

Ethan had built the fire near to the trail, figuring that the risk of Buck's men finding them was worth taking if it brought a traveller to them. And the small, grizzled man they'd attracted was definitely not a member of Buck's group.

'Friend,' the man hollered, 'am I welcome?'

'You sure are,' Ethan hollered back and beckoned the man to ride into the camp.

The man pulled his wagon up before the fire, then jumped down and joined them.

'I'm Mulcahy Jones,' he said.

'I'm Ethan and this is Amelia.'

Mulcahy glanced at Amelia, his gaze lingering longer than was polite. Ethan judged that he was sizing up whether she was his daughter or his wife.

'You travelling with your granddaughter?' Mulcahy asked.

Amelia snorted a low laugh.

'No,' Ethan grunted.

Mulcahy raised a hand. 'No offence meant. Just you got such a young wife.'

Amelia coughed, unable to get out any words.

'No offence taken,' Ethan said. 'Please, share our warmth.'

As Amelia continued to splutter and dart glares at Ethan, Mulcahy glanced around the campsite. From his raised eyebrows, Ethan reckoned he'd already noticed their lack of horses or baggage.

'I guess you ain't got no food on you either,' he said.

'We haven't.'

Mulcahy smiled. 'Then it's a good job that I have.'

Mulcahy only provided them with a mess of beans and a lump of stale bread, but they produced one of the finest meals Ethan had ever tasted.

When they'd eaten, Mulcahy passed around a whiskey bottle. Amelia declined and after a moment's thought, Ethan did, too. This persuaded Mulcahy to give up trying to encourage conversation and he retired to sleep a respectful distance away from them.

'Why did you say we were married?' Amelia asked when they'd settled down beneath their only cover, the horse blanket.

'I didn't,' Ethan said. 'I just didn't argue with him.'

'Why?'

'Because an attractive young woman like you will get a whole heap less unwanted attention if everyone thinks we're together.'

Despite the warmth of the fire, beneath her blanket, Amelia shivered.

'That still didn't stop him leering at me.'

'Can't blame him for that.' Ethan tugged the blanket up to his chin. 'But he knows that if he approaches my *wife*, he'll face trouble.'

'I am not your wife,' Amelia intoned, then turned her back on Ethan and dragged the blanket off him.

'Yeah, yeah,' Ethan murmured, struggling to grab the blanket back, 'now go to sleep, dear.'

Amelia slapped his arm, but Ethan shuffled back to slip under the blanket again, although he did manage to avoid his back touching her back and, with a smile on his lips, let sleep grab him.

In the morning, Mulcahy's bustling woke him and he joined him to chat amiably before he left. But when Mulcahy had his wagon ready to move on out, he broached the subject that he'd avoided so far.

'We're heading to Green Valley,' he said, 'and we'd be much obliged if you'd take us there.'

'Normally I'd be accommodating,' Mulcahy said. 'But Green Valley is fifty miles that-a-way.' He paced out to point down the trail, then swung his hand over his shoulder to point in the opposite direction. 'And I'm heading that-a-way.'

As Ethan winced, Amelia joined them.

'We will pay you to take us,' she said.

'How much?'

Amelia drew Ethan back a pace. 'How much money do you have?'

'The river took everything. But I still have the money I won off Leach, perhaps thirty-five dollars.'

Amelia nodded and turned to face Mulcahy.

'We'll pay you thir—'

'Ten dollars,' Ethan shouted.

'Nope,' Mulcahy said. 'That ain't worth my while. I got some trading to do in Bear Pass.'

Amelia glanced at Ethan, her eyes wide in what Ethan took as silent encouragement to increase his offer, but Ethan mouthed back that they had to pay for train tickets in Green Valley.

'Please,' Amelia said, turning to Mulcahy and smiling. Then she took a deep breath and fluttered her long eyelashes. 'Please.'

'Well . . .' Mulcahy rubbed his bristled chin. 'All right. I'll take you half-way there for ten dollars.'

'Half-way is very generous of you.' She laid a hand on his arm. 'But all the way would be better.'

'And,' Ethan said, 'you'll avoid the trouble. An outlaw, Buck Lincoln, raided Bear Pass and killed a whole heap of people.'

'Trouble, you say?' Mulcahy grinned. 'In that case, I'll take you half-way there for twenty dollars. When there's trouble, my prices go up and I can't afford to not get to Bear Pass by sundown.'

'Twenty dollars it is,' Amelia said. 'Pay the man, Mr Craig.'

'Yes, dear,' Ethan murmured and slapped bills into Mulcahy's hand.

Mulcahy created a space for them in the back of his wagon and they trundled down on to the trail then swung round to head towards Green Valley.

'I'm almost out of money now,' Ethan grumbled.

'As you've said before: we'll worry about that problem later. For now, we aren't walking.' Amelia raised a foot, then slipped out of her boot and massaged the sole of her foot. 'And I am thankful for that.'

Ethan managed a begrudging nod. 'I guess I am, too. Seems we're back on schedule to get you wed.'

'We are.' She cleared her throat. 'And if you don't mind me asking, have you ever been married, Mr Cr . . . Ethan?'

'I have – twice.' Ethan stared forwards, watching the trail disappear behind the trundling wagon, then turned to her. 'First wife died. The second . . . Well, we're no longer together.'

'I am sorry to hear that.'

'Got two children, but haven't seen them in a while.'

'Where are they?'

Ethan gathered a handful of dried corn-husks from the bottom of the wagon and juggled them in his hand.

'A town in the south called Dirtwood.'

'Couldn't you return to see them?'

64

Ethan began throwing the husks over the side of the wagon.

'I was doing just that when you distracted me with this here journey.'

Amelia winced. 'I'm sorry again.'

'Don't be.' Ethan flashed a smile. 'I guess I needed an excuse. I don't reckon I'll be welcome.'

'The parting was bad?'

'It was.' Ethan hurled the last husk as far as he could, then batted his hands clean. 'Martha forbade me from doing something and I went ahead and did it anyhow. Afterwards, things weren't the same and it wasn't long before I left. And now I'm divorced on the grounds of abandonment for one year.'

'That is too bad.'

'I learnt plenty from the mistakes I made, mind. Before, I was bull-headed and inflexible, but now I'm more relaxed and just go where the fancy takes me.'

Amelia stared at him, perhaps encouraging him to offer more with her silence, but Ethan found he didn't want to discuss a private concern that'd plagued him for the last few years. Presently, she turned to join him in sitting on the back of the wagon with her feet dangling over the side.

Every so often, they crested a hill and this let him see the route over which they'd travelled and, each time, the river had faded further into the distance until, at last, it disappeared.

After travelling all morning at a steady pace, Ethan reckoned they must have covered over half the distance to Green Valley. But he didn't head to the front to mention this to Mulcahy, not wanting to risk drawing his attention to the fact that he'd taken them further than promised.

The sun was beginning to drop when Mulcahy drew the wagon to a halt. They alighted.

Amelia tried to bargain for more miles, even simpering and cajoling Mulcahy in a manner Ethan would never had expected when he first met her. But Mulcahy was determined to get to Bear Pass before sundown and left them in a hurry. Although he did give them a small parcel of salted pork and a heel of bread.

With no choice, they resumed their journey to Green Valley on foot.

But unlike their tramping yesterday, they now covered distance at a healthy rate, walking beside a trail with their bellies full and their bodies rested. And every time they crested a new high point, Ethan looked ahead with hope that he might see Green Valley ahead, then back to see if he could see another traveller.

But he saw neither and the sun was dipping when the weariness again descended on them.

Amelia's wedding was on the day after tomorrow in White Creek, but even with that deadline approaching, they agreed that they wouldn't reach Green Valley tonight.

So, they settled down in an elevated position, one hundred yards off the trail, aiming to rest for the night, then start walking early and reach Green Valley as soon as they could tomorrow.

Amelia didn't know when the train was due, and if they missed it, they would need to be lucky enough to arrange another way of getting to White Creek.

With neither of them feeling that luck was a commodity they had in abundance, they settled down for the night, eating their small parcel of food, then settling down beside the low camp-fire.

They hadn't spoken much all day, and now weariness overcame them quickly. Ethan had guarded their camp-fire, not encouraging any night meetings. He judged that the likelihood of Buck Lincoln finding a way across the river was growing with every passing hour.

Sleep was claiming him when he heard hollering down on the trail, then the clop of hoofs as at least one rider headed towards them.

Ethan silently cursed himself for not letting the fire die out, then drew his gun and sat back against a boulder facing down the slope. When the newcomers stopped, he saw that there were two men. Amelia had also snapped awake and shuffled back to lie beside him.

'You folks mind if we share your heat?' one man said.

'Come into the light and I'll decide,' Ethan said.

The lead rider nodded and paced into the circle of firelight. The second rider stayed back but was close enough for Ethan to see the features of both men. They were young, with eager but gap-toothed grins and arrogant stances. Neither had any baggage and their sweat-slickened horses were panting.

'What you decided, stranger?'

'You can stay.'

Amelia flashed a warning glance at him, but Ethan

winked, trying to convey that having them where he could see them was better than wondering where they were.

'You offering your name?' the man asked.

'The name's . . . John McGiver.'

'And the woman?'

'I'm his wife,' Amelia said before Ethan could speak.

CHAPTER 7

The man looked around the campsite.

'Now what's a man and his *wife* doing out here without horses?' he asked, then grinned, his teeth bright in the firelight.

'It is not polite to ask questions of strangers,' Amelia said.

The man twitched back, mock indignation registering on his smirking face.

'And that ain't a welcoming attitude.'

'Just settle down over there,' Ethan said, gesturing with his gun towards a clear area some ten feet from the fire. 'We got no food to share, only heat, and pleasant conversation if you're minded.'

'I *was* minded, but that there wife of yours just ain't friendly.'

'She is friendly,' Ethan grunted. 'So, where are you heading?'

Both men stood side by side. One man spat into the fire, the other grinned.

'White Creek.'

'Yeah,' the other man said. 'We got a celebration to go to.'

Ethan nodded. 'What celebration?'

'Some say it'll be a wedding.' The man chuckled. 'But we reckon it'll be a funeral.'

The man continued to laugh as he glanced at his companion, but then whirled his hand to his holster, but even before the gun cleared leather, Ethan had slammed a quick shot into the man's chest that hurled him backwards. Even before he'd hit the ground, Ethan had delivered a scything shot into the second man's arm that spun him to his knees and half-around. A second slug in the back sent him sprawling face down into the dirt.

Then Ethan was on his feet and running for the men's horses. He secured their reins, breathing a sigh of relief as he gained them, then peered into the darkness, his hand raised to Amelia for quiet. But he heard nothing but the wind.

He led the horses back to Amelia, then kicked out the fire. Within moments, they were both on the horses and heading down to the trail.

'You recognize them?' Ethan asked.

'No.' She pointed ahead. 'But are you sure we should head to the trail?'

'The rest of Buck Lincoln's men must be searching for us, but this late, I reckon they'll have holed up, and this is our best chance yet of getting to Green Valley fast.'

Amelia offered no more objections and despite the horses' tiredness, they managed a reasonable pace as they headed down the trail, the late gibbous moon rising to light their way.

Through the evening they rode steadily, all the

time looking out for lights or listening for noises that'd herald them happening across Buck Lincoln or his men. But they neither saw nor heard anything untoward and after two hours of steady riding, they saw a subdued grouping of lights ahead, which as they emerged from the trees revealed itself to be Green Valley.

The town was sleeping, not a person being out, although when they pulled up outside the only hotel, a light was on inside.

Amelia stared wistfully at the upstairs windows.

'Can we spare enough money to stay here?' she asked.

'Got no idea how much the tickets to White Creek will cost, so it'd better if we didn't.'

'But still, to sleep in a bed would revive my spirits.'

Ethan nodded. 'All right. I reckon we can get a bed for the night for a dollar. I'll knock them up.'

Amelia jumped on the spot, even clapping her hands, but as Ethan walked past her, she flinched, then moved to stand before him.

'*A* bed,' she said, 'and *we?*'

'Yeah. We can't afford two beds. And don't worry, as you know, I don't snore.'

She stamped her foot on the boardwalk. 'We are not sleeping in the same bed.'

'Well I ain't paying no dollar a night to sit in no chair or on no floor.'

'You will not be sleeping in the same room.'

Ethan set his hands on his hips. 'Why is that different to what we've done for the last two nights?'

'It just is.' Amelia swung round and stomped down

71

the road. 'Come on. We will sleep at the station.'

'We won't get no two rooms there,' Ethan shouted after her, but she had built up a good pace and he had to run to keep up with her.

After a night in which Amelia lay on a bench at the station with her head resting on her rolled-up wedding dress, and Ethan lay on the platform, they awoke to find the ticket collector opening his office.

'Wake up,' Ethan said, nudging Amelia's arm. 'It's the day before your wedding day.'

Amelia sat, then stretched with her eyes still closed.

'And I never thought that day would start like this.' She looked up to see the ticket collector join them.

'You're mighty keen to get that train,' he said.

'Yeah,' Ethan said, suppressing a yawn. 'When is it?'

'Be here within the hour. You want tickets?'

Ethan glanced at Amelia, who opened an eye and provided a sleepy nod. Ethan bought two tickets for White Creek, and was surprised to be still left with a few dollars. After they'd gone over the waterfall, Amelia had promised to compensate him for his losses, but strangely, still having money in his pocket comforted him.

For the first time, he started to think that he would get Amelia to her wedding without any more mishaps. With a lightening step, he paced around the station. Presently, other passengers arrived to await the train, but they all gave them a wide berth.

Ethan watched and when yet another person made an obvious attempt to stand away from them, he stepped back and looked Amelia up and down and then himself. He sighed.

They had accumulated far more than the usual trail dirt. Grime encrusted their clothing. Amelia's repeated brushing through undergrowth had converted her skirt below the knees to ragged lengths of cloth.

Amelia stared at him, then saw what was concerning him and sat. She fussed with her clothing, but didn't improve a look that only a complete change of clothing would aid.

'Don't worry,' Ethan said, sitting beside her. 'You're still a mighty fine-looking woman.'

'And that is the least convincing thing you've said to me. I don't know what Wesley will say when he sees me arriving like this.'

Ethan nudged her and winked. 'If he's any kind of man, he'll just be pleased to see you.'

'I hope so, but I also hope I can have a bath before he does.'

'Your skin ain't that dirty.'

'The skin is not the problem.' She sniffed. 'The smell is.'

Ethan sniffed deeply. 'I can't smell anything.'

Amelia matched his deep inhalation. 'Neither can I. And that's the problem.'

Ethan flashed a smile, but then stood. As Amelia continued to fuss over her clothing, he sniffed himself, then shrugged and stood waiting for the train.

An hour after sun-up, right on time, the train arrived with much accompanying excitement from not only the awaiting passengers, but also the citizens of Green Valley, who emerged on to the road to wave the train in.

Ethan asked about the excitement and learned that this was the only train this week. Their good fortune in being here to meet it cheered Ethan even more and suggested that maybe their troubles were behind them.

They boarded the train last and sat apart from the other passengers. They both sat with their backs held straight, but when the train moved out, they both relaxed and enjoyed watching the landscape pass. By degrees, the steady shaking of the train even lulled Ethan to sleep.

They faced another three stops before they arrived in White Creek, a journey of some eight hours. The first two stops passed quickly, but the journey to the third was lengthy. But as they swung round to head down into Rawbone, Amelia brightened and even pointed out the River Green nestling in the trees ahead.

Ethan sat bolt upright. They had seen only two men from Buck's group and that implied the gang had split up to search for them. And as Green Valley then Rawbone were the next places for an easy river crossing, it was likely that some of Buck's men would have headed down here to intercept them. Ethan kept these thoughts to himself, but as the train pulled into the station, he saw the line of men standing on the platform.

Amelia was already ducking, and Ethan slipped down in his seat, but stayed high enough to watch the line of men file towards the train, two cars down from them.

'Is that them?' she asked.

'Yeah,' he said. 'Buck Lincoln and his men are getting on the train.'

CHAPTER 8

Ethan stood and ushered Amelia to walk down the aisle and away from the car into which Buck and his men had climbed. By the time they reached the door, the train was already lurching to a start, but it still wasn't travelling so fast that they couldn't jump off.

'You reckon we should stay on?' Amelia asked as they slipped through the door.

Ethan glanced through the window in the door. Buck had to be searching for them, but he didn't know that for sure, and there was still a chance he didn't know they were on the train.

'Yeah. He'll see us if we get off. We need to hide.'

With Ethan leading, they worked back through the cars until they reached the last one, which, from the surly expression of the conductor who stood before it, was probably the baggage-car and not for the passengers' use.

'What you want?' the conductor asked.

Ethan peered over the conductor's shoulder, seeing the dusty and darkened interior, and plenty of stacked crates and other promising places where they could hide.

He smiled. 'We weren't comfortable. We thought we'd stay here.'

'You did, did you?' The conductor eyed Ethan, then glanced at Amelia. 'Well, I ain't letting you sit in here. So, unless you got some baggage you want to see, you can turn around and head back to your seat.'

Ethan rubbed his chin as he searched for a valid reason to go inside, but Amelia stood beside him.

'In that case,' she said, 'we have some baggage we'd like to see.'

The conductor narrowed his eyes. 'What kind of baggage?'

'If I knew that, I wouldn't want to see it.'

The conductor stared at her, but Amelia returned a firm-jawed glare, which, along with her steady foot tapping, said she wasn't in the mood for answering questions and further delays would not result in a quiet life.

With a shrug, the conductor stood aside and directed them to enter. But he followed them in and stood by the door, eyeing their progress down the aisle.

'I didn't expect you to lie so well,' Ethan whispered.

'Perhaps that is the influence of several days spent in your company.'

'I'm glad you've learnt something from me. But—'

'You found that baggage yet?' the conductor shouted from the door.

'Yeah,' Ethan said, then pointed at the stack of crates in the corner. 'It's over there.'

'Those crates ain't yours.' The conductor paced towards them, his eyes gleaming with the self-belief that he now had enough evidence to prove they were engaged in a suspicious act. 'They're a delivery for a Mr Sinclair.'

'Are you sure?' Ethan said. He wrapped his arms around either side of the nearest crate and moved to lift it, but no matter how much he strained and braced his back, the crate stayed precisely where it was.

'Yeah. And unless you reckon you can lift a ton of iron, I wouldn't try and move that.'

'Then I won't.' Ethan stood, wincing at the sound of his back creaking into place, then pointed through a gap in the crates. 'But I reckon our baggage is behind here.'

'Ain't nothing behind these crates.'

'Even better.'

Ethan climbed on to the first layer of crates and peered over the second layer to see that aside from a broken crate and some rags a space was beyond, some ten feet square set before the closed double-doors.

'You happy that it ain't there now?'

'Nope.' Ethan lowered a hand to Amelia, who hitched up her skirts then climbed the crates and swung up on to the top layer. She glanced over the side then threw down her wedding-dress.

'And just what do you think you're doing?' the conductor muttered.

Ethan ignored him as he helped Amelia to jump down on to the other side, then swung up to sit on the topmost crate.

'What I am doing is putting my hand in my pocket. Then I'm taking my hand out.' Ethan fingered through his remaining bills, then peeled off a one-dollar bill. 'And I'm giving you this.'

The conductor's hand drifted towards the bill, but then he snatched it back.

'I don't accept bribes.'

'I ain't negotiating. One dollar is all I'm offering.'

'You don't listen. I ain't interested in no bribe no matter how high.'

Ethan stared down at the conductor, wondering how he'd managed to find the only honest conductor on the railroad, then smiled.

'We don't want anything from you, and we ain't looking to steal anything. We just want you to leave us alone, for one dollar.' Ethan thrust out the money again and waved it above the conductor's head.

The conductor watched the bill wave back and forth, then tore his gaze away from the enticing money and centred it back on Ethan.

'And why should I leave you alone? Because there ain't nothing behind there but . . .' The conductor's mouth fell open. Then he clamped it shut, but as Ethan returned a slow wink, a huge grin appeared. 'Oh, I see. You want some time together in private.'

Amelia jumped up from behind the crates.

'We do not,' she screeched before Ethan lunged down and slammed a hand over her mouth, then waggled his eyebrows at the conductor.

'And as you can see, she's mighty frisky and keen for that private time.' Ethan lowered the bill for the conductor to swipe it from his grasp. 'Be obliged if you left us now.'

'No problem, no problem at all.' The conductor rocked his head from side to side as he peered through a gap in the crates, his wistful gaze perhaps searching for another glance at Amelia, then shrugged and headed back to the door.

Ethan jumped down from the crate and, despite Amelia's struggling, kept his hand clamped over her mouth until he heard the conductor close the door. Then he lifted his hand, but in return received a stinging slap to the cheek.

'I have tolerated many indignities at your hand,' she muttered, colour rising on her cheeks, 'but you will not imply that you and I are . . . are . . .'

'The conductor just accepted my bribe so we'd have some time in private to talk.' Ethan pouted his bottom lip in a feigned hurt expression. 'What did you think I was implying?'

'You implied that we would be . . . would be consorting.' Amelia stared at the huge grin that Ethan couldn't stop breaking out. 'Oh, you are just a filthy-minded man.'

'But you were the one who thought I meant something else. You must have learned some interesting things at Mrs Haversham's school for young ladies.'

Amelia slapped her hands on her hips, but then turned away to glance around their new hiding-place.

'Anyhow,' she said, her voice gruff, 'you appear to

have acquired us a place to hide.'

Ethan stared at Amelia's back, wondering how to raise another laugh from her discomfort, then shrugged and paced around, looking for how they could maximize their chances of staying hidden. He again tried to move the crates to make a more secure space, but the heavy iron ensured he couldn't move them at all.

The crates surrounded double doors and Ethan peered through the gap in the doors, then dragged them a few inches to the side, confirming that they weren't locked, then slammed them shut.

He piled the remnants of the broken crate in the corner, then draped the rags over the wood. He stood back, but judged that they wouldn't cover them both.

'Perhaps the dark will help us,' Amelia said.

'Perhaps it will, but I hope Buck won't find us in the first place.'

But then the conductor started talking to some-one in the doorway. They both strained their hear-ing, and Amelia murmured confirmation that the other man was Buck and, from the low tones, he was trying to get past the conductor.

Ethan grabbed the doors and dragged them open to gain a two-foot gap. The wind whipped in, but he glanced outside, then up towards the roof. But when he darted back in, Amelia was shaking her head.

'We can't jump. That'll kill us.'

'It might. But I was just giving us an option, and making it appear that the doors were always open.'

'That's a bad idea. Close the doors and don't let so much light in.'

Ethan wavered, but judged that the corner where they planned to hide was still dark enough to hide them from a casual observer.

Then a loud slap sounded, followed by the heavy thud of a body hitting the floor. Down the aisle, the door opened and footfalls sounded as at least three men came in.

'Search everywhere,' Buck shouted.

'You can't come in here,' the conductor whined.

'If you want another slap, say that again.'

'But there's—'

A slap sounded, then a heavy thud of a fist pounding into flesh. The conductor grunted and pleaded for his assailant to stop, but two more heavy blows sounded.

'Now, have you got any objection to us coming in here?'

'I have,' the conductor bleated, 'and there's still nobody in here.'

'And what's makes you think I'm looking for someone?'

'You've been searching in all the cars.'

'I guess I have.' A loud clatter sounded, then glass breaking, then another clatter. 'And now I'm searching in here.'

Ethan motioned for Amelia to hide under the rags, then edged to the widest gap in the crates and peered through. At the end of the aisle, Buck had hoisted the conductor up and slammed him back against the wall. Two of his hardcases were rifling through a box and systematically dropping or smashing whatever they found.

'They ain't in here,' one hardcase said with harsh laughter in his voice, then threw the box aside and opened a second box. 'Let's see if they're in this one.'

'What you reckon?' Buck asked. 'Will he find them in there, or will he end up smashing everything again.'

'I can't tell you nothing,' the conductor said, then swung his head to the side and peered straight down the aisle of crates and boxes at Ethan.

In the poor light, Ethan reckoned that he wouldn't be able to see him, but the conductor continued to stare at him.

'Then I guess we'll just have to search this box.'

Buck nodded and his hardcase removed a vase then hurled it to the floor, but the conductor continued to stare at Ethan's position.

'You didn't listen,' he urged. 'I can't say where the people you're looking for are.'

'Then you'll . . .' Buck stared at the conductor. Then, with a snap of his wrist, released him and swung round to face down the aisle.

Ethan edged back from the gap, then joined Amelia under the rags. They pressed themselves flat against the crates, trusting that the poor light would help them.

Footfalls paced down the aisle towards them, then stopped on the other side of the crates. Then the crates shook as someone climbed them. From above him, Ethan heard breathing as that person peered over the side.

'See anything?' Buck asked from the other side of the crates.

'No, but it's dark.' The crates shook again as Ethan assumed that the man clambered on top of the crates, then a heavy thud as he leapt down to land on their side.

Ethan nudged Amelia and pointed to the doors, then hurled the rags from him and leapt to his feet. In two long paces he was on the man. He swung him round, then thundered a blow to his chin that slammed him back into the crates. The man's head piled into the solid iron and he slid to the floor, unconscious.

Amelia had taken Ethan's hint and was already standing by the doors. Ethan backed across the space to stand beside her, his gun drawn and aimed at the top of the crates ready to take whichever person risked coming over the top.

But a face peered through a gap in the crates. Ethan blasted a shot that slipped through the gap and ricocheted away over the man's head, but it forced him to dart back.

'It is them,' that man shouted.

Then another man bobbed up over the crates, but Ethan ripped lead at him and forced him to dive for cover.

'Get the rest,' Buck shouted. 'We've got them trapped and they just ain't going nowhere.'

Ethan glanced at Amelia, receiving a worried frown in return, then glanced through the open doors. Beyond, the rocky ground hurtled by fast enough to deliver a whole heap of broken bones to anyone who risked leaping from the train.

With nobody else risking coming over the crates,

Ethan leant back to peer outside, then jumped up. His trailing fingers brushed the roof.

He nodded towards the door handle and, despite Amelia's raised eyebrows and the shake of her head, pointed at the roof with a firm finger.

Amelia followed his gaze, then looked towards the crates behind which Buck was murmuring orders. Then the door opened at the end of the baggage-car and, with a deep breath, Amelia gathered up her wedding-dress and slung it over her shoulder. She lifted her left foot to the door-handle. Ethan clamped a hand under her right foot and lifted her off the floor.

She kept hold of the side of the door and reached up. Ethan watched her and, when her foot inched from the handle and she swung out, he realized she'd found something to grab hold of outside.

He grabbed her trailing foot then levered her up and, with surprising speed, she swung up and out, then disappeared from his view. Ethan took careful aim at the gap in the crates, then fired two quick shots through it.

Scuffling sounded as Buck's men dropped to the floor, while Ethan thrust the gun in its holster and matched Amelia's actions. And, as he swung out he saw that she'd grabbed hold of a hook that dangled above the doors and used that to lever herself up on to the roof.

Amelia herself was kneeling on the roof and was reaching down towards Ethan, but her hand was two feet above his head and Ethan didn't fancy her chances of being able to drag him up without pulling them both down. Instead, he put all his weight on the door-handle, then lunged for the hook.

The hook held and he dangled for a moment, then risked releasing a hand to slap it on top of the roof. He levered himself up a foot, but then his limited traction failed and the hand and then his body slipped down the side of the train.

Within the train, clattering sounded as Buck's men climbed up the crates, but from the steady muttering of orders, Ethan guessed that they still hadn't realized he and Amelia were trying to escape.

He lunged again. And again he couldn't find a grip, but this time, Amelia grabbed his wrist and pulled. She also slipped along the roof towards him and Ethan flashed her a glare that told her to release him or risk being pulled from the train. But with a return flashed glare, Amelia refused his offer, then braced both her feet against the thin rim of the roof and tugged. Ethan felt his body lift.

He decided to risk lunging with his other hand, then put all his efforts into one long swing. He had a moment of weightlessness, then looped a foot over the rim of the roof and dangled, suspended, half his body on the roof, the other half dangling. Then his weight toppled him sideways to roll on to the roof, entangling himself with Amelia before they rolled to a halt.

'Obliged,' he said.

Amelia smiled but then pointed down the roof. Ethan nodded and with her at his side, they scurried down the roof top.

The train was now arcing on a long approach to a

bridge over a river, the drop to the water below more than a hundred foot. Behind them, Buck's irritated cries emerged from the open door indicating he'd discovered they'd gone. But by then they'd reached the end of the baggage car.

Ethan looked at Amelia to ask whether she could jump to the next car, but she'd already hitched her skirts above the knee, and was hurrying to the gap.

She leapt, landing lightly a good two feet on, and Ethan followed, but he stumbled as he landed and went to his knees.

He caught his breath as he rolled to his feet, but a gunshot ripped past his left shoulder from behind. As he started running, he looked back to see Buck and his men piling out of the baggage-car, but then they disappeared from view as he pounded after Amelia.

She reached the end of the next car ten paces ahead of him, jumped, then carried on. Ethan followed her, but as he landed, he heard shouting from behind and he risked looking back. Two men were venturing up on to the roof, but Ethan fired at them, forcing them to duck.

Ethan ran sideways, firing as he ran, but with the increased distance, the men risked rolling out on to the roof, and Ethan acknowledged he wouldn't be able to keep them at bay. He hurried on after Amelia. She stopped, having jumped on to the last car, and stood waiting for him, beckoning him on with sharp gestures.

As Ethan hurried on to join her, he searched for but could find no solution to the problem of what they did now. As far as he could tell, Buck's men no longer had them trapped at one end of the train – they had them trapped at the other end.

Below them, the rattling of the train intensified as they trundled over the bridge and, for a crazy moment, Ethan peered over the side of the train wondering whether they could survive the drop to the water below. He dismissed that wild idea from his mind, but, looking ahead, another crazy idea came to him. It felt possible.

'What are we doing?' Amelia shouted.

'We head down into the last car.'

'And then what?'

'I have a plan, but it'll take too long to explain.'

Amelia nodded and moved for the ladder at the side of the car. The men behind were now only one car away. Ethan hunkered down with his gun trained on the men, who slowed and stayed back, waiting until they had back-up.

When Amelia jumped down off the ladder, Ethan slipped down the ladder after her.

'I reckon,' she said, 'that you'd better do whatever it is you're planning to do. And do it quickly.'

Ethan glanced through the window in the door. Buck was leading a row of men down the central aisle. He darted his head back, then peered around the side of the car, seeing that the engine was now leaving the bridge.

'The plan is just one word.'

'Which is?'

Ethan watched the last bars of the bridge pass as the train returned to firm ground.

'Jump.'

'Jump?'

'Yeah, jump!'

Amelia stared at Ethan, her mouth falling open. But then she nodded, thrust out her hand for him to grab it, and began a countdown from three.

But Ethan heard the door swing open behind him. He ripped his hand away, then slapped a firm hand in the centre of Amelia's back, wheeling her from the train. Then he flexed his knees and, with a silent prayer, jumped after her.

CHAPTER 9

Ethan and Amelia flopped to a sprawling halt on a stretch of sand beside the bridge with Ethan lying flat on his back and Amelia lying on his chest. Ethan stared at the sky, gritting his teeth after the bone-jarring fall and mentally checking his body for injuries.

Finding nothing beyond an all-over numbness, he looked up to see Amelia lifting herself up from him with her hair dangling.

He held her chin and considered her face to see that aside from her blinking away the shock, she didn't appear to be in pain.

'I'm fine,' she murmured. 'Except I am closer to you than I ever planned to be.'

Ethan glanced down to see how entangled their limbs were, then provided an embarrassed smile. He tried to roll her off him, except she rolled in the same direction and he only succeeded in tipping her over and landing on top of her.

'Sorry,' he murmured.

'Mr Craig,' she said, staring up at him with her

eyes wide, 'would you please get off me.'

'I'm trying,' Ethan murmured, pushing himself up with arms that shook so much that he flopped back down on her.

'Then try harder!'

Ethan shrugged, then squirmed himself off her and, to avoid looking her in the eye, crawled towards the tracks and peered down them to see the last train-car disappearing in a long arc around a hill. A smile was just tugging at his lips when a gunshot whistled by his left ear.

He threw himself flat, judging that the shooter was close and was down the tracks. Then he saw the twisted mound of a body, about twenty yards away, of someone who hadn't been so lucky in his leap from the train.

He searched for the other shooter, but then a man bobbed up from behind the body and ripped lead at him. The shot cannoned off the tracks beside his head. Ethan rolled to the side to lie in the centre of the tracks and waited, with his body presenting the smallest possible target and his elbows planted in a firm triangle.

A minute passed before the man risked bobbing up, but he never got the chance to fire as Ethan winged a high shot into his chest that rocked him back on his haunches. A second shot flattened him.

Then Ethan rolled off the tracks and scurried away. Amelia had hidden behind the nearest cover, the main stanchion of the bridge, and he joined her, finding that from there, he could see down the tracks and defend her against anyone else who came from that direction.

For fifteen minutes they waited, but nobody emerged and by then, both Amelia and Ethan were feeling more composed after their leap. With Ethan now accepting that they were safe here, he looked at Amelia.

'I reckon Buck will get off the train to ambush us somewhere,' he said. 'So, I ask again: how badly do you want to get to White Creek today?'

Amelia peered down the tracks. 'I want to wed tomorrow, but I guess if I'm late for my wedding, it could still all work out.'

Ethan sighed as he rubbed his chin. 'Let me get this straight. If you wed tomorrow, you inherit, and you and Wesley share your father's ranch?'

'Yes.'

'But if we hole up, Wesley will search for you when you don't arrive on the train. Even if it takes him a week to find you, you and he can still wed, and with your uncle owning your ranch, he'll have to give it to you?'

'That is right.'

'And you're sure he'll do that?'

Amelia narrowed her eyes. 'I do not like what you're implying. My uncle is an honourable man.'

'I ain't implying nothing. I'm just trying to make the right decision to save your life. Now, are you sure nothing changes? Will he pass the ranch on to his son and new daughter?'

'Of course.' She shrugged. 'Although Wesley's brothers might—'

'Brothers! You never mentioned them.'

'They aren't dangerous. Seth is the eldest and Cullen is the youngest. And they are both sweet young men.'

'Sweet young men when you left maybe, but what about now?' Ethan blew out his cheeks as she shook her head. 'If they can stop you reaching White Creek, they could inherit a share of your father's ranch, and are you telling me that couldn't tempt them?'

Amelia bristled, but she didn't look at him as she paced back and forth, swaying her wedding-dress before her.

'I don't think they would harm their future sister-in-law.'

'But it is possible?'

She looked up and met his gaze. 'Anything is possible. And I suppose they could have hired Buck Lincoln to stop me getting to White Creek.'

'Then I got no choice but to ensure you do get there today.' Ethan slapped Amelia's shoulder and pointed her down the tracks. 'Come on. Get that chin up and start smiling. You're getting wed tomorrow.'

Amelia wandered a slow pace. 'But I have nothing to smile about. If I miss my wedding, I lose everything. And if I wed, I have to tell Wesley that his brothers have tried to kill me.'

Ethan and Amelia walked throughout the hot afternoon. The train-tracks followed a straight enough course, letting them see well ahead, but they saw no sign of Buck. This did not cheer Ethan, suggesting to him that he had found a good place to ambush them.

And, as the day wore on, he realized that they wouldn't reach White Creek by sundown, and that when they did meet Buck, they would not be in a fit state to mount a defence.

Ethan estimated they had walked for fifteen miles since jumping off the train, and had more than that to travel, when he saw the first building since leaving Rawbone. It was a squat building beside the track, perhaps an abandoned station, but as they closed, Ethan saw a new buckboard outside the building and he decided it was a trading post.

As only one horse was mooching in the corral outside, they went inside and were faced by the yawning post-owner.

'Train don't stop here no more,' he said with the bored indifference of someone who provided that answer at least once a day.

'We don't want the train,' Ethan said. 'We want your help.'

'Then you've come to the right place.' The post-owner grinned and turned on the spot, drawing their attention to his mouldering wares that clogged every available inch of space in the building. 'What do you want?'

'We want to hire your buckboard.'

'Ain't for hire.'

'We can pay.'

The post-owner narrowed his eyes. 'How much?'

Ethan fished in his pocket and prised out the sum total of his wealth. He slapped the bills and coins on the counter, then fingered them apart to count them.

'We can pay you the sum total of four dollars and fifty-five cents.'

'That ain't enough.'

'Then I'll pay you five hundred dollars,' Amelia said, slapping her palm on the counter.

The post-owner stood back to look her up and down, his attention staying on the tattered remnants of her skirt.

'You ain't got nothing more than four dollars and fifty-five cents.'

'My name is Amelia Ash and I am marrying Wesley Lister tomorrow if it is the last thing I do and you will give me your buckboard and Ethan will drive it to White Creek and tomorrow one of Wesley's ranch hands will return the buckboard to you with five hundred dollars. Is that clear?'

The post-owner gulped. 'Yes, ma'am.'

With a swing of her tattered skirt and her wedding-dress thrown over her shoulder, Amelia marched out of the post.

'I reckon you were right sensible when you agreed to that,' Ethan said, then winked at the post-owner.

At a steady pace, they headed down the trail. Ethan had taken the post-owner's advice to follow a seldom-used and circuitous route which would still get them to White Creek before sundown, but which would let them arrive from an unexpected direction.

They saw nobody on this trail and after thirty miles, after which they were still ten miles from

White Creek, Ethan started to feel that they might arrive safely.

Amelia even started to relax, pointing out familiar landmarks with a relaxed air as if their traumatic journey had never happened. Seven miles out of White Creek, she directed them to a trail that would take them to her uncle's ranch, but it was only then that Ethan saw three riders approaching from ahead. These men were slowing to a halt, and from the side, two other riders were closing in to join them.

'You recognize them?' Ethan asked.

'Not yet,' Amelia said, narrowing her eyes, then winced, 'but the man on the end was definitely on the train.'

Ethan drove on, but slowed the horse and, from the corners of his eyes, looked around. The plains were flat and lacked cover. The trail was otherwise deserted. Their only defence was their closeness to their destination and the certainty that gunfire would attract helpful attention.

'You ready for this?' Ethan asked.

'I've come this far.' She shuffled her wedding-dress on to her lap. 'These men won't stop me.'

'My feelings exactly.' Ethan shook the reins and they drove on. 'We'll keep going at this pace, and when we reckon they're ready to make a move, we'll speed and go straight through them.'

'I trust you to succeed, Ethan.'

'I will. And just so you know, I . . .'

'Know what?'

Ethan glanced at her and discovered that he couldn't form the words to convey what he wanted to say.

'I guess I'm trying to say that I reckoned time spent with a woman who'd been to Mrs Haversham's school for young ladies would be an ordeal. But you're right pleasant company and one hell of a resourceful woman. And when Wesley sees you in that wedding-dress, he'll know he's the luckiest man alive.'

'I'd like some of that luck now because those men aren't moving.'

Ahead, the men had grouped to block their way, but Ethan kept going at the same pace, trusting that as Buck wasn't amongst them, they'd lack the authority to know what to do without orders.

They were fifty yards away when one man nudged his horse forward.

'Howdy,' he shouted, 'we're here to escort Amelia to the Bar J.'

'A likely story,' Amelia murmured beside Ethan. 'Keep going.'

The lead man watched them ride closer. He glanced back at the other men, receiving a wave of shrugs. One man edged his hand towards his gunbelt, but the lead man shook his head then turned.

'I said,' he yelled, 'we're here to—'

With a great roar, Ethan shook the reins and hurtled the horse on towards them. The riders stood for a moment, but then the buckboard blasted straight through their centre, scattering the men in its wake.

Ethan encouraged the horse to greater speed as he heard the men shouting orders at each other to regroup. Galloping hoofs closed on them from behind. Then the first gunshot whistled over his head and he thrust the reins into Amelia's hand, then turned in his seat and vaulted into the back of the buckboard. He hunkered down and, with his stance steady, fired back.

His first shot tore the nearest man from his horse, but this encouraged the others to swing out and flank them.

Then five more riders thundered out from a tangle of boulders, about fifty yards away, and arced in towards them. Buck Lincoln was in their midst and he was heading straight for the buckboard with his gun brandished.

CHAPTER 10

One of the pursuing men swung in to the side, then leapt on to the back of the buckboard, grabbing Ethan around the neck as he slammed into him.

But Ethan rolled with the blow and danced back, letting the man's momentum throw himself over the side of the buckboard. The force almost dragged Ethan with him, but Ethan grabbed hold of the side of the buckboard then righted himself.

He turned, but it was to face another man leaping on to the buckboard, and this man landed lightly, only stumbling to one knee before he steadied his stance. Ethan ripped up his arm, but before he could fire, another man slammed into his back and ground him into the timbers.

On the bottom of the buckboard he floundered, feeling both men pressing their weights on to his back.

Then cold metal stabbed into the base of his neck. He flexed, aiming to try one desperate attempt to buck the men, but then the weight lifted and Ethan was sliding to the front of the buckboard.

He hit the back of the seat, but both the men who were holding him flew over the side. Ethan realized that Amelia had yanked back on the reins and slammed down the brake lever, stopping the buckboard in a skidding halt within yards.

Ethan stumbled over the seat, his body falling for a moment, but then Amelia shook the reins and they lurched off again.

The sudden movement swung him back on to the buckboard. The wheels bumped and lurched as they trundled over at least one of the fallen men, then they were off and heading on towards the ranch again.

Ethan stood and, for the first time, saw the ranch looming ahead, but from his glance, he saw no sign of anyone noticing the phalanx of riders heading down the trail.

Another volley of shots ripped into the side of the buckboard, one bullet tearing across Ethan's trouser leg and leaving a flap of cloth. Ethan winced even though the bullet had missed skin, then threw himself flat to lie behind the side boards and peer over.

Now he took careful aim and winged the nearest trailing rider from his horse, then tore a second shot into another man's leg, snapping him back in the saddle before he pulled his horse to a halt.

Ethan risked glancing around and saw that he'd reduced the numbers of riders down to just four men, but these men charged on ahead, swinging round to block their route.

'Keep going,' Ethan shouted, 'no matter what they do.'

'I intend to,' Amelia shouted, but then shrieked.

Ethan stood and saw that one of the riders had taken the daring move of leaping off his horse and on to the buckboard's horse. He was waving his arms as he fought for balance, but then swung round to sit upright and his dragging on the horse's bit encouraged the horse to slow.

Ethan rolled into the front of the buckboard, but even though they were less than a mile from the ranch, the rider was slowing the horse to a trot. Ethan aimed his gun at the man's back, but a warning shot tore past his arm and a glance to the side confirmed that their pursuers had him in their sights. And he had no choice but to raise his hands and let the man drag the buckboard to a shuddering halt.

'What are we going to do?' Amelia asked.

'Delay them,' Ethan whispered. 'Somebody at the ranch has to have heard this.'

Amelia nodded then turned to look at Buck.

'Why are you after me?' she asked with her voice low and calm.

'You don't ask the questions,' Buck said. 'Now, you will turn around and head back the way you came.'

'I won't. But you will state your business. Then I will leave.'

'There's only one thing you're doing.'

'I know.' Amelia passed the reins to Ethan, then raised her rolled up wedding-dress from her lap. 'I am wearing this tomorrow.'

Buck glanced at the wedding-dress and snorted, but Amelia teased out a length of the dirtied cloth, then opened up the remainder of the dress. She held it high, showing the dress to the row of riders, who all sneered. But then hot fire ripped out through the cloth as she pumped a bullet from a concealed gun into the man on the buckboard's horse.

The shot was ill-directed and only winged his arm, but it was enough to rock him to the side, and a firm shake of the reins from Ethan lurched him all the way to the ground.

Ethan used the momentary confusion to blast a slug into one of Buck's men and then they were off, heading towards the ranch.

'How long you had that gun?' Ethan shouted, passing the reins to Amelia.

'Got it from one of the men who attacked us at the camp-fire. Thought the surprise might be useful.'

Ethan nodded then glanced back to see that Buck and the only other rider were about twenty yards back, but swinging in towards them. He ducked as a bullet hurtled past his head then swung round on the seat and knelt. With one eye closed, he took careful aim at Buck, but his finger twitch fell on an empty chamber. He grimaced then lunged for Amelia's wedding-dress and rummaged through the cloth to get to the six-shooter.

He wasted valuable seconds searching for the gun, and by the time he'd dragged it clear, he heard a thud behind him. He turned to see that Buck had jumped on to the back of the buckboard and was pacing along it.

Buck raised his gun to aim it at Amelia's back and, at their side, the other man was swinging in, his arm arcing round to aim his gun at Amelia. Ethan jumped to his feet and vaulted into the back of the buckboard.

He fired sideways, his fright-induced senses heightened enough to wing a shot into the rider's guts and blast him from his horse. Then he was running at Buck.

He fired on the run. The shot was wild, but, caught in a moment of indecision, Buck wavered then turned his gun on Ethan. At the moment he fired, Ethan leapt through the air and wrapped his arms around Buck's chest, knocking him to the timbers. Both men skidded on their sides as they ploughed into the back boards.

Another gunshot ripped out, the blast burning between them and rippling heat across Ethan's stomach. He and Buck stared into each other's eyes, both sharing a moment when neither man knew who had been hit.

Then Buck rocked back, his arm clutched across his chest. He rolled to his knees, then staggered to his feet to stare over the back of the buckboard. From the bottom of the buckboard, Ethan looked up, watching him stagger round on the spot.

'Why?' he asked.

Buck shrugged, then flexed his arm and tugged his gun up to aim it at Amelia, but Ethan blasted a shot into his chest, wheeling him from the back of the buckboard.

As they trundled through the ranch gates, he stood and peered over the side to see Buck's body flop to a halt five yards beyond the ranch perimeter.

And at regular intervals behind lay the bodies of his unsuccessful fellow-ambushers.

Ethan turned and headed to the front of the buck-board, rolling into the seat just as Amelia pulled it to a halt before the ranch house. Through the windows and over by the bunkhouse, Ethan detected movement, and within moments, he expected Amelia to disappear into the warmth of her family and friends.

He turned to her and smiled and, in a gesture he hadn't expected, she threw her arms around his neck and brushed his cheek with a kiss.

'I can never thank you enough for getting me here,' she whispered in his ear.

'That was all the thanks I needed.' Ethan extricated himself from her arms. 'Now, don't give your sweetheart any cause to get the wrong idea.'

Amelia nodded and jumped down from the buck-board with her wedding-dress clutched to her chest.

With the kiss still burning Ethan's cheek far more than the bullets that had nearly hit him did, Ethan jumped down and stood beside her, facing the ranch.

An imposing gentleman emerged first, his wide-eyed and open-mouthed expression a mixture of joy and shock. From the way Amelia jumped on the spot, Ethan guessed this was her uncle, Frank Lister.

Amelia held her arms wide and Frank paced down the ranch steps to face her. Lurking in the shadows behind him other people milled, looking at her with bemusement, too.

Then one of the men noticed the body of Buck Lincoln beyond the gates, and within seconds, people were hurrying around them. But in the midst of the confusion, Amelia and Frank just smiled at each other, then paced towards each other and embraced.

Then Frank held her back to look her up and down.

'I reckon,' he said, 'you have a tale to tell.'

'I do. And I am not looking my best.' Amelia tucked an errant strand of hair behind her ear, but then held the wedding-dress aloft. 'But at least my wedding-dress survived.'

Frank eyed the ripped and dirt-coated garment.

'I don't know why you bothered,' he murmured.

CHAPTER 11

'If Wesley's here,' Amelia said, 'I don't want him to see me looking like this.'

'He's in town,' Frank said, 'and will be until you're wed.'

She smiled, then paced back to stand beside Ethan.

'And I will be, thanks to Ethan.'

Frank tipped his hat to Ethan, then ushered them both to head to the ranch house.

'What happened to Leach Oldrich?' he asked.

'He decided not to come to the Bar J,' Ethan said. He stopped in the doorway and looked back to the gates where several of Frank's ranch hands were peering down at Buck's body. 'As did a whole heap of men lying dead back along the trail.'

'Dead! Why?'

'Somebody hired them to stop Amelia getting here.'

Frank paced into his ranch, shaking his head.

'Can't see why anybody would want to do that.'

'Buck Lincoln was the ringleader.'

'Ah, that varmint. I just knew I'd have trouble from him again. Wesley and the boys couldn't get any reliable work out of him.' Frank sighed and patted Amelia's shoulder. 'So, I had to run him off your father's ranch, but he never took advice well. He hung around, tried rustling, and I guess you were the obvious next choice for his anger.'

'Is that why you hired Leach to protect me?' Amelia asked.

'No. I never expected Buck to go after you. If I had, I'd have collected you myself.'

Amelia put a hand to her heart. 'Then I am pleased.'

'You're pleased that Buck wanted to kill you!'

'I've spent the last few days wondering why anyone would want to stop me wedding your Wesley, and—'

Frank raised an imperious hand. 'And you don't need to say anything more. I understand your concern, but you got nothing to worry about here. Buck Lincoln was a man with a mission, and I'm just pleased you had a decent man with you like Ethan to stop him completing it.'

As Amelia nodded, Ethan paced round to stand before Frank.

'And you got no reason to suspect that anything else was behind his mission?' he asked.

'Like I said, you got nothing to worry about here. If Buck was after her, the problem begins and ends with Buck. I'll get my hands to scout around. They're familiar with the people Buck counted as friends and they'll make sure they aren't around.'

Amelia started on another round of questions, but

Frank considered Amelia's grime-coated face and clothes, then the trail of dirt she'd made from the door. He put a finger to his lips, then clamped a hand on her shoulder and directed her towards a corridor that led from the main room to what Ethan presumed were the bedrooms.

This time, Amelia relented and after sharing a last glance with Ethan, she left them. Both Frank and Ethan watched her leave, but she stopped by the corner and turned.

'One last thing,' she said, 'we have one more guest for the wedding.' Amelia looked at Ethan and smiled. 'If you're minded to stay another day.'

'Nobody can stop me being there,' Ethan said.

Amelia nodded, then left the room. Ethan watched her leave and continued to stare in her direction after she'd left, but then realized that Frank was looking him.

'You did well,' Frank said.

'Despite everything, it was a pleasure to get her here.'

'I'm sure it was.' Frank eyed him while rubbing his jaw, then went to a cabinet by the wall, which he unlocked, then returned with a wad of bills. 'And I'm sure you must have incurred a lot of expenses, so we'll get this over with now.'

He counted bills into Ethan's hand, but then shrugged and slapped the whole lot down.

'Obliged,' Ethan said, closing his hand on what he reckoned was more than twice as much as the most he'd expected to receive.

'We got a lot of family and friends staying tonight

so you can't stay here, but the Hotel Splendour in town will see you right.'

Ethan had no problem with that arrangement and made his farewells quickly. Frank headed outside with him to organize his hands into rounding up the bodies strewn back along the trail. Ethan was minded to help, but now that his task was complete, weariness and a desire for a peaceful time overcame him, so he left them to do whatever they needed to do.

He borrowed a horse from the ranch, then headed into town.

White Creek was already well into its early evening bustle, but Ethan squeezed into the general store just before it closed and purchased a complete change of clothes. Then he headed across the road to the barber's, which was closed.

But he knocked up the barber, then paid double, without complaint, for a shave, a trim and a bath filled with skin-burning hot water and lashings of every smelly fragrance the barber could provide. He couldn't remember the last time he'd pampered himself so much, but for reasons he couldn't resolve, he felt a need to do it now.

Then he booked into the hotel and lay on the bed, staring at the ceiling. Despite the crisp feeling of his new clothes and the tingling of his skin, he was bone-weary, but he still had to will sleep upon himself. And it just wouldn't come, a restlessness and a growing desire to move on forcing him to roll off the bed and pace back and forth.

Perhaps the forthcoming wedding or maybe the enforced closeness with Amelia had returned his thoughts to family, but whatever the reason, he decided that he now did want to seek out his kin after the wedding.

He looked through the window, then dragged it open. Raucous singing and general merriment drifted in through the window and that did it for him. He slapped his hat on his head, headed out of the hotel, and hurried to the Silver Horseshoe for a celebratory drink or ten.

Around him, the saloon was lively and, from the snippets of conversation he listened to, most of the customers were in town for the wedding or lived here and were using the wedding as an excuse for their revelry. Many people tried to gather him into companionable chatter, but he rebuffed the offers with a friendly smile and settled back against the bar to enjoy everyone else's enjoyment.

From the chat he did join in with, he learnt that the two men who were dancing and carousing with four saloon-girls at the base of the stairs were Wesley's younger brothers, Seth and Cullen. After his recent suspicions, Ethan eyed them. Although he decided they were vying with everyone else in the saloon to prove they were the drunkest and most boisterous, he detected only youthful exuberance and a desire to celebrate their brother's impending marriage.

He didn't see Wesley, so when the next person, Pete, tried to drag him into conversation, he pointed to the boys.

'Lister boys are having fun,' he said.

'They sure are,' Pete said, 'but it ain't every day

110

that the two biggest ranches in the county get themselves together.'

'I guess it ain't. Where's Wesley?'

Ethan's new friend licked his lips and waggled his eyebrows.

'He ain't here.'

Pete's grin suggested that Ethan ought to know where he was, but when Ethan just returned a shrug, Pete laughed, slapped him on the back, and leaned over the bar to grab a whiskey bottle.

For the next half-hour, his new-found drinking buddy pummelled him for information about why he was in town. And after Ethan had provided the answer, he questioned him about how he knew Amelia.

Despite being contented now to accept that no sinister surprises awaited him before the wedding, Ethan deflected Pete's questions and spun a story about knowing her from her time at Mrs Haversham's school for young ladies. The sheer unlikeliness of this lie forced him to change the subject frequently and spend more time questioning Pete about his own life, but then a loud cheer sounded in the saloon.

Ethan turned to see a man striding down the stairs from the rooms upstairs. He had a saloon-girl on each arm, and both women were wiggling their hips as they descended and were waving to the crowd in the saloon below to encourage their catcalls.

When the group reached the bottom, the two Lister brothers whistled and bellowed at the man. Then Seth pushed the saloon-girl who had been sitting on his knee towards him.

The girl sashayed towards the newcomer, then pointed up the stairs.

The man shook his head, then mopped his brow in a parody of being too tired, but to a chorus of encouragement, he let her grab his hand and drag him a pace towards the stairs.

Then he dug his heels in, but she released his hand and fell to her knees on the bottom step. She thrust out her hands in mock pleading and, to another round of whistling, the man relented with a short bow and let the woman lead him back up the stairs. But not before he'd swiped a whiskey bottle from the nearest table.

Ethan watched them lurch up the stairs, the man pausing to throw back his head and pour a good slug of whiskey down his open mouth. But the saloon-girl tugged him away from the bottle and dragged him up the stairs. More rank encouragement from the Lister brothers hastened him on his way.

Ethan turned to Pete, who laughed as he leaned back on the bar.

'Now, Ethan,' he said, '*that* is Wesley Lister.'

CHAPTER 12

Lying on his bed, Ethan stared at the ceiling of his hotel room, trying to force sleep upon his tired body. But his mind was still whirling after what he'd witnessed in the saloon.

Amelia's betrothed had not only taken a string of saloon-girls upstairs, but had later boasted about his activities and, from the girls' and his brothers' reactions, his behaviour was typical and was something he was inclined to continue.

In the past, Ethan had witnessed plenty of carousing before weddings and he'd sure had nights to remember before he got wed – although he couldn't remember either of them.

But Ethan, like everyone he considered to be a decent person, knew the boundaries of acceptable behaviour. He guessed that Wesley's privileged background had instilled in him a belief that his drunken and licentious behaviour was acceptable. But Wesley had pushed the boundaries of decency for any man, and especially for one who was about to marry a young woman whom he'd come to admire like Amelia Ash.

This was not Ethan's problem. As soon as the wedding was over, he intended to head back to Dirtwood and risk seeing the children he hadn't seen for the last three years. But even after only a few days with Amelia, he felt a bond with her that he didn't like to question too much.

And that bond said he had to do something, or at least say something. But everything he could do or say wouldn't make things any easier for her.

His biggest inclination was to have a stiff talk with Wesley, but such talks only worked when the recipient respected you. Neither did he know Frank well enough to discuss this with him, and from the open way Wesley behaved, it was possible that he might see nothing wrong in his behaviour.

That left Amelia. One word from him would stop her marrying Wesley, but losing her inheritance would hardly improve her life.

The answer refused to come before he slept, nor when he awoke to pace around his room, nor when he strolled around White Creek at sun-up.

Feeling far less enthusiastic about the joyous occasion than he'd thought he would, he sat in the hotel watching people come and go until it was time for the wedding. Then he headed out to the Bar J ranch, quickly mingling with a trail of guests, many of whom he recognized from last night, and all of whom were in high enough spirits to wave at him whether they recognized him or not.

At the ranch gates, he joined a queue. Two ranch hands were waving everyone through, but when it was Ethan's turn to file in, the hands stood before his horse.

'Sorry,' the nearest hand said, 'we ain't doing nothing today but have ourselves a wedding. You'll have to come back tomorrow.'

'I am here for the wedding,' Ethan said.

'It's only invited guests.'

'I am an invited guest.'

The hand sighed with a deepness that suggested this wasn't the first time today that he'd had to deal with this embarrassing situation.

'And I'm sure whoever invited you last night was being right friendly, but they also had no right to do that. I'm afraid you'll have to celebrate for us elsewhere.'

Ethan maintained his fixed smile. 'Amelia invited me yesterday.'

'Amelia invited you,' the hand intoned. 'And that was in the few minutes she had free when she arrived from the school, was it?'

'I was the one who escorted her from the school.'

The hand blinked with momentary confusion, then drew the other hand aside. They shared a whispered conversation. Then the second hand scurried off to the ranch.

'While we check on that, would you mind waiting over there?'

'I guess I can wait,' Ethan murmured then headed in the direction the hand had pointed.

He dismounted by the bunkhouse and leaned against the wall. There, he watched the guests continue to file in, none of them suffering the level of questioning that he had suffered.

But then he saw Wesley's elder brother, Seth, heading towards him from the ranch house. He pushed himself from the wall to stand before him.

'You're the man who helped our Amelia get here?' Seth asked.

'I sure am,' Ethan said, standing tall and preparing for the congratulations.

Seth nodded as Ethan heard footsteps pace around the bunkhouse then towards him from behind, then they quickened and Seth's eyes flicked up to look over Ethan's shoulder. Ethan swirled round but it was to see two men charging at him. He just had time to throw up an arm, but then they threw a sack over his head.

He struggled, but the men crammed the sack down his body then threw him back against the wall. Ethan struggled, trying to hurl the sack from him, but a solid blow to the guts winded him, a crack to the side of the head knocked him to his knees, and a firm boot on his back flattened him.

Someone dragged him to his knees and removed his gun, then wrapped a rope around his waist and pulled it tight, pinning his arms to his side. Then rough hands lifted him to his feet and marched him away.

Ethan shouted, trying to attract the guests' attention, but his assailants speeded their journey and within ten paces, Ethan slammed into a horse. Then they swung him over the horse and, within seconds, they were riding off, with Ethan lying sideways with his head and legs dangling over the horse.

Aside from the occasional barked instruction, Ethan heard nothing but the clop of hoofs and had no idea where his bushwhackers were taking him, but he judged that they had travelled about three miles when the horse halted. His assailants dragged him down from the horse and threw him on his back, then tugged the sack from his head while still keeping the rope around him that encased his arms.

Ethan blinked against the sudden brightness, then peered up to see three men standing over him. One of the men was Seth. He didn't recognize the others, but they appraised him with the arrogant gazes of men used to violence and used to being given orders.

Seth walked these men back a few paces and muttered low orders. Ethan didn't hear everything they said, but overheard enough to learn that his other captors were Hicks and Salmon. And he also learnt that the main debate wasn't about what they should do with him, but as to where they should dump his body.

Then Seth turned and, without another look at Ethan, mounted his horse and rode away. Ethan watched him leave, noting the direction of the Bar J ranch for, he hoped, his future use, but Salmon grabbed the rope that pinned his arms to his side and dragged him to his feet.

Ethan stood tall and raised his chin.

'I heard those orders,' he said, 'but you'd be wise to ignore them.'

Salmon cracked his knuckles. 'Why?'

'I'm a lawman,' Ethan said, firming his jaw and trying to appear honest. 'And killing a lawman is mighty serious.'

'You're right. That does change everything.'

Salmon chuckled, then spat a huge gob of spit in Ethan's face. As it oozed down his face, he pulled a knife from his belt. 'Now we ain't just going to kill you, we'll have ourselves some fun first.'

Salmon advanced on Ethan, his knife rising towards Ethan's face. Then he darted it forward. Ethan snapped his head to the side, the knife slicing through a dangling strand of hair.

Salmon thrust in again, Ethan again shuffling back, but this time Salmon's move was a feint and he pulled the knife back and considered Ethan. Then he gestured over his shoulder at Hicks for him to hold Ethan still.

Hicks paced around Ethan, giving him a wide berth, then moved in. With Hicks advancing on him from behind and Salmon standing before him, Ethan stood tall, searching for the moment he could try to escape, and knowing he'd have to find that moment soon.

But just as Hicks moved to grab his arms, Salmon transferred the knife to his left hand and wiped his sweaty palm on his jacket. This was the best opening Ethan reckoned he'd get and he charged Salmon, who saw Ethan's intent and thrust up the knife, but he wasn't quick enough. Leading with his shoulder, Ethan barged into him and knocked him back three paces.

But Salmon dug a heel in and stopped his sliding, then sliced the knife up, aiming for Ethan's face, but Ethan swayed back from the blow, the knife whistling through the air before his nose.

Then, as Salmon floundered, he kicked his legs

from under him and leapt on him. Hicks was only feet behind him, but Ethan had kept his gaze on the knife and even with his arms held firmly at his side, he wrapped a hand around the hilt, then yanked the knife from Salmon's grip.

To evade Hicks he rolled over Salmon then, lying sideways, thrust the knife against Salmon's back, hard enough to slice through the cloth, but not hard enough to break skin.

'Stop right there,' he grunted, 'or I'll slice him in two before you can shoot me.'

Hicks slid to a halt and glared down at them, his gun drawn and aimed at Ethan's exposed head, but a desperate whine from Salmon encouraged him to stand back. But he stopped five paces away and stared at them.

'We got ourselves a problem then, because I got a gun on you and you ain't leaving here alive.'

Ethan slapped his other hand on Salmon's side then, keeping a firm grip, ordered him to get to his feet. Slowly, they rose together, Ethan not daring any sudden movement or Salmon would get away from his short arm-reach.

When they were standing, he swung Salmon round to stand before him, but kept the knife jabbing in his back. With his other hand, he moved towards Salmon's holster, but Salmon detected his intent and spooned the gun out on to the ground.

'What you going to do now, then?' Salmon said, forcing a laugh despite the knife digging into his back.

'Now,' Ethan said, 'your friend is going to throw down his gun.'

'I ain't doing nothing you say,' Hicks grunted.

'You hear that, Salmon,' Ethan muttered in Salmon's ear. 'Your partner is all set to get you killed.'

As this truth filtered into Salmon's mind and he started fidgeting, Ethan used the moment to slip the knife back and into his other hand, then jab an extended finger into Salmon's back. With the knife held back, he began a steady sawing motion on the rope binding his arms to his waist.

'He's right,' Salmon said, staring at Hicks. 'You ain't getting me killed here.'

'And we got our orders.'

As Salmon and Hicks glared at each other, Ethan sawed with more haste, judging the moment when they lost patience with the situation as being close. The bonds frayed, then split, but the motion attracted Salmon's attention.

Salmon squirmed, but then grunted, probably as he realized that there was no longer a knife in his back. He turned, but at that moment, the last of the rope fell away from Ethan's waist and even before the rope hit the ground, Ethan danced back a pace, steadied his stance, then hurled the knife.

The knife flew through the air, shining like a silver bullet as it circled towards Hicks then sliced into his guts, embedding itself to the hilt. Hicks staggered back, the gun falling from his fingers as he clutched the knife, then toppled backwards.

Weaponless now, Ethan clipped Salmon under the chin, then followed through with a long blow to the cheek that whirled Salmon to the ground. But Salmon landed near to his gun. He rolled, then grabbed it, and Ethan had no choice but to run and leap on him.

The two men rolled over each other, the gun pressed between them, but then their struggling squirmed the gun out. Salmon strained to aim it down at Ethan's head. He squeezed out a shot, the blast hot as it hurtled by Ethan's right ear. The gun was still closing in on Ethan's head as Salmon used his superior strength to drag it towards him.

Ethan strained again, halting Salmon's progress, but then released his hand. The gun snapped to the side, swinging past Ethan's head. Ethan darted his head forward, slamming his forehead into Salmon's face and flattening his nose.

Salmon squawked as his head rocked back, but Ethan took advantage of his pained shock and grabbed his gun arm, then bent it at the elbow and thrust the gun up under Salmon's chin. A solitary shot ripped out.

As Salmon tumbled backwards, Ethan wrested Salmon's gun from his dying grip, then checked on Hicks, confirming that he was just about breathing his last. He lay him on his back, but Hicks had enough strength to shrug away. So, Ethan located his gun and hurled it over his shoulder, then hunkered down beside him.

'You going to tell me what this is all about?' he asked.

'I ain't saying nothing,' Hicks murmured, a bubble of blood on his lips.

'But are all the brothers behind this? Are they planning to kill Amelia before the wedding to get her father's ranch?'

'You won't stop nothing.'

Ethan questioned Hicks some more, but although he received no answers, it let him voice the fears that had plagued him ever since Amelia had recognized Buck Lincoln. If Amelia only inherited when she wed, finding who had the most to gain from stopping that wedding would confirm who had hired Buck. And now it was clear to Ethan that Amelia wouldn't live long enough to marry a man who wasn't even worthy of her.

And Ethan was also clear as to what he had to do.

He left Hicks to die alone, then mounted his horse and followed the direction in which Seth had left to return to the Bar J ranch and the location of a wedding that wouldn't be the happiest day of Amelia's life.

The ranch was quiet as Ethan approached. The guests had all entered and, from the subdued music playing within, Ethan judged that the wedding ceremony was close to starting.

He rode through the gates unchallenged and pulled up outside the bunkhouse, then paced to the ranch house, keeping on the lookout for anyone waiting outside. He saw nobody. Before the doors, he waited, listening to the music playing within, then hurled open the doors to stand framed in the doorway holding on to each door.

He faced the backs of the rows of guests. Down the central aisle, he saw Amelia in her newly cleaned and mended wedding-dress standing beside Wesley and facing the minister, the Reverend Matthew Johnson.

Only Matthew looked at Ethan, but with a flick of his eyes, he signified that Ethan should sit and not interrupt them.

Ethan nodded and closed the doors behind him.

Matthew coughed. 'This is an occasion in which the word of God—'

'The word of God means nothing here today,' Ethan said in a clear voice that echoed through the room.

As one, all heads turned to look at Ethan.

In his few moments of orientating himself, Ethan had located Wesley's younger brothers sitting on the front row. Both these men jumped to their feet. A ripple of other guests stood to block his sight of them, but Ethan was able to confirm the brothers were not packing guns.

'What are you doing?' Frank said, pacing into the aisle. 'You cannot interrupt my son's wedding.'

'I ain't interrupting this farce,' Ethan said, planting his legs wide and drawing his gun. 'I'm stopping it.'

CHAPTER 13

All the wedding guests shouted at once, but Ethan kept his gaze on Amelia, trying to convey the seriousness of the danger she was in, but Wesley stood before her.

'You cannot stop this,' he shouted, his voice loud enough to reduce everyone else's shouting, and when he had silence, he repeated his demand.

Ethan glanced around the guests, seeing many of the people who had witnessed Wesley's activities in the saloon last night and even two of the saloon-girls.

'Perhaps I can't, but I can ask Amelia a question.'

'You are not—'

'Please,' Amelia said, edging Wesley aside, 'let him ask. I have come to trust Ethan with my life, and if he needs to ask a question, I want to hear it.'

'Thank you,' Ethan said. He paced down the aisle, but stopped half-way down so that the brothers were all before him. 'Do you know what Wesley was doing last night?'

Wesley paled, but Amelia just gave a sly smile.

'I know that he was celebrating in the saloon.'

'And do you know that he was . . . was consorting with saloon-girls.'

'Con . . .' Amelia swirled round to face Wesley. 'Tell me that isn't true.'

'It isn't true,' Wesley murmured looking over her head.

'Look me in the eye and say that.'

'Amelia,' he said, still not lowering his gaze, 'you have to trust me.'

'Don't!' Ethan shouted. 'That man ain't worthy of you. He's everything that a woman like you despises in a man.'

'Why are you saying these things?' Amelia pleaded, turning to Ethan.

'Because they're true and because Wesley's brothers have just tried to kill me. They *do* want your father's ranch, and you won't live to see the end of the day and claim your inheritance.'

'You can't be . . .' Amelia opened and closed her mouth but everybody started shouting and Ethan didn't hear her words.

Wesley swirled round to face his brothers. Frank staggered back and had to grab a chair to stop himself falling over, but Ethan thrust his gun high and blasted a single shot into the ceiling, silencing the sudden rise in noise.

'I am telling the truth and Amelia is leaving this here ranch with me, unwed and alive, and if anyone tries to stop us, they'll need the minister to send them on their way to the next life. Now, everyone keep their hands where I can see them and let us leave peaceably.'

Ethan stared down the aisle at Amelia, who glared at Wesley, beseeching him with her watering eyes to deny Ethan's claim, but Wesley just stood with his head lolling and murmuring to himself. Then he creaked his head up to glance at her before looking over her shoulder.

'None of this is true,' he murmured.

'Don't believe him,' Ethan urged.

'I have to believe my future husband,' Amelia said. She looked at the Bible in the minister's hand, and Matthew handed her the book. 'But Wesley isn't my husband yet and he will swear on the Bible that none of this is true.'

With a tentative gesture, Wesley reached for the Bible, flinched back, then laid a hand on it.

'I could never harm you,' he said. 'And I know nothing about my brothers trying to harm you or Ethan either, and if they are, I will kill them where they stand. I swear that.'

'I believe you.' Amelia took a deep breath. 'Now, tell me about last night.'

Wesley gulped. 'I . . . I . . . I can't remember much about last night. I'd had a lot to drink and . . .'

'And?'

'And I can't remember.' Wesley looked away, his hand slipping from the Bible.

'You *can* remember and you *will* tell me.'

Wesley swiped a bead of sweat from his brow, then clasped his hands together, but he still looked over Amelia's head, his gaze picking out one of the saloon-girls.

'You've been gone for five years and I was lonely,

but all that is—'

'Then it is true,' Amelia shrieked.

Wesley gave the barest of nods before Amelia screeched and drew back the Bible, then slapped him across the cheek with it, sending him to his knees. Then she lifted the heavy book high above her head and slammed it down again and again on his head and shoulders, knocking him first one way then the other.

Wesley threw up a hand to defend himself but Amelia's berserk rage knocked the hand away. Only when he fell on his back and the Bible's cover flew off did she throw the book down on his chest.

'Read that. And when you work out where you went wrong, beg forgiveness, but not from me.' Amelia hitched her wedding-dress to her knees and, in one huge stride, paced over Wesley's body then down the aisle towards Ethan. 'Come on. Get me out of here.'

And with that, she flounced down the aisle, then sobbed and hurried past Ethan and outside.

Ethan paced backwards still keeping his gun on the front row in case either of the brothers turned on him, but he reached the door with everyone still standing transfixed. He stood in the open doorway, then slammed the doors shut behind him and looked around for Amelia, not seeing her for a moment. Then she arrived, having commandeered a buggy.

She dragged the buggy to a halt outside the ranch door and, without encouragement, Ethan jumped on the seat.

'That was supposed to be the happiest day of my life,' she said, her voice catching.

'I'm sorry,' Ethan murmured. 'But there's one good thing to come out of this – you look beautiful in that wedding-dress now it's all mended.'

Amelia forced a thin smile, then, with a crack of the whip, turned the buggy in a short circle. And by the time the guests piled out of the ranch behind them, they were away through the gates.

'And what do I do now?' Amelia asked.

'I got no idea,' Ethan said. He paced across the blackened earth and looked through the remnants of the window at the plains and the mountains on the horizon.

Amelia had driven them from the Bar J ranch at a good pace, and although Ethan hadn't questioned her, he'd guessed where she would go. He'd spent the journey constantly looking over his shoulder for a pursuit that had to come, but they'd reached Amelia's old family ranch without seeing anyone.

The place was a burnt-out wreck; the fire, followed by five years of the elements, had reduced it to a shell, but even so, Ethan could tell that it had once been a well-built and loved building.

'But,' she said, her voice tired and distant, 'you must have thought what you'd do after you'd burst into my wedding.'

'Nope. I just dealt with the big problem first and figured we'd work out what to do after that.'

'And now?'

Ethan kicked the base of the wall. 'And now I wish

there was something I could say that'd make this easier.'

'You could tell me why Wesley did it for a start.'

'I've seen plenty of people do plenty of stupid things, myself included, but I still have as much idea as to why anyone does them now as I ever had.'

Amelia sighed. 'But you don't need to worry. You did the right thing to save my life.'

'Not sure now that I did save your life. I was when I burst in there, but I reckon I now know what the plan was.'

'Which was?'

'Seth and Cullen hired Buck Lincoln to kill you. When that failed, they devised a second plan. They ensured everyone saw Wesley con . . . doing what he did in the saloon. Then I reckon one of the saloon-girls was going to jump up and announce what happened before you wed.'

Amelia nodded. 'Then I'd stop the wedding myself, and Frank would disown his son for what he did.'

'And Seth and Cullen would get a whole ranch between them.'

Amelia joined Ethan at the window. 'Their greed doesn't excuse Wesley's actions.'

'It doesn't, but perhaps they led him astray and encouraged—'

She swirled round to face him, her eyes blazing.

'I can't believe you're defending him.'

'I'm not. I just reckon I understand what happened. And I reckon you know that, too.' Ethan watched as Amelia provided the shortest of nods.

'But even if he was led astray, I cannot forgive him.' She sighed. 'And I am now out of time. In a few hours, I will lose my father's ranch.'

'Frank looked as shocked as you were. Perhaps you can talk to him and he might gift it to you.'

'He might,' she murmured.

Ethan patted her shoulder. 'I can see you're as suspicious as I am about everyone now. I'm sorry I did that to you.'

'Don't be.' She nudged out from beneath his hand. 'But now, leave me. I need time alone.'

Ethan turned and paced to the fallen length of wall where the door used to be, but he stopped with a hand holding on to a burnt and standing length of timber doorframe.

'You do realize it's also likely that Seth and Cullen killed your brother in this very house.'

'I am aware of that.'

'Then you won't mind if I wait around nearby, will you?'

'I would like that. And I will call for you when I am ready to leave.'

Ethan raised his foot to leave the building, then lowered it. He opened and closed his mouth twice, wondering whether to mention the wild thought that had just hit him, then shrugged and did it anyhow.

'You have to be wed by the end of the day,' he said, turning, but not able to look at her, 'to inherit your father's ranch, right?'

'That is still my biggest problem.'

Ethan coughed, still looking away from Amelia.

'And to be wed you need a man.'

Amelia snorted a harsh laugh. 'I thought I had found the right man, but I hardly think I can cram the ten years that it took Wesley and me to be nearly wed into less than eight hours.'

'Perhaps you don't have to.' Ethan edged from foot to foot. 'You don't need to find a husband before midnight. You just need to find a man.'

'I suppose so,' Amelia murmured, 'but where would I find someone willing to wed me in the next few hours?'

Ethan removed his hat, looked up to face her, and smiled.

CHAPTER 14

Amelia pulled the buggy up outside the lawyer's office in White Creek.

'This is still,' she said, 'the most ridiculous idea I've ever heard.'

Ethan threw his hands wide. 'I ain't arguing with that.'

The few people out on the road had stopped to stare at her, but she hitched up her wedding-dress and jumped down on to the boardwalk without waiting for Ethan to help her get down. She looked up at him.

'Then I guess we'd better do this before I start thinking straight.'

Amelia strode into the office, trailing Ethan in her wake.

The lawyer looked up from the tangle of papers that were on his desk and frowned on seeing Amelia advancing on him. Ethan smiled when he realized that this man was Matthew Johnson, the minister who had presided over her aborted wedding ceremony.

'I am so sorry it didn't work out,' Matthew said,

pointing at the papers. 'But I rushed straight back after the wedding and started work. I've found nothing yet to challenge your father's will, but—'

'But you have nothing that will work within the next few hours,' she said.

Matthew winced, rocking his head from side to side, but then provided a short nod.

'I haven't, but that won't stop me looking.'

'Then stop looking. There is no problem no more.' Amelia gulped and took a deep breath. She glanced at Ethan, who closed the door behind him and joined her. 'I intend to be wed within the next five minutes.'

Matthew raised his eyebrows. 'You've changed your mind about Wesley?'

'I most definitely have not. I have a new . . .' Amelia sighed deeply and looked aloft. 'Who am I trying to convince? This *is* a ridiculous idea. When I marry, I will marry for love, not for land.'

Ethan placed a hand on her shoulder. 'And you will do, one day. But we're just sorting out the current problem. Then you can worry about the rest later.'

'I know, but this is too much.' She swirled round to face him. 'I mean, marrying you. I can't think of anything more preposterous.'

As Matthew flinched so hard his glasses fell off his nose, Ethan snorted.

'I made Martha a fine husband and I assure you—'

'Oh, I am sorry, Mr Craig. I never meant that the idea of a woman wanting to marry you was preposterous, but that woman isn't me.'

As Ethan searched for the right words to convince her, Matthew raised a hand and coughed.

'Are you telling me,' he said, delivering each word with a tone he probably reserved for courtroom interrogations, 'that you've decided to marry the first man you can find to get around this problem with the will?'

Amelia shook her head, but Ethan nodded.

'She has,' he said. 'I have no desire to be wed and no desire to own her father's ranch. All I want is to get this over with and let her, and me, get on with our lives.'

'You will not speak for me,' Amelia snapped, 'not even if you were my husband.' She stamped her foot. 'I know my own mind, and I will not marry you.'

'It is a solution,' Matthew said, his glazed eyes suggesting he hadn't heard Amelia's declaration, 'and it's better than any of the ideas I've come up with.'

Ethan turned to her. 'There you go. It's a solution. So, will you marry me?'

'I wouldn't marry you if you were—'

'If I were the only man who could give you everything you want?'

Amelia swirled round to look away from both men, who both took the moment to glance at each other and exchange a nod.

'If you put it like that,' Amelia murmured, 'I reckon we should just get wed. And do it quick, Mr Johnson, before I start thinking again.'

Matthew fished in his desk for a Bible, then stood. Amelia and Ethan stood side by side, but several feet apart and, despite the falseness of the situation, Ethan smoothed his hair, then buttoned his jacket. And after a moment's thought, he unhooked his gunbelt and threw it on the desk, then lifted the knife he'd taken from Salmon and clattered that down on the desk.

Amelia, for her part, indicated that both men should turn their backs. They did and a rustle, then a clatter sounded as she threw a concealed gun on the desk.

Ethan couldn't stop a smile from emerging as he turned back to watch her smooth her dress, then play it out around her.

'You still look beautiful in that dress,' he said.

'And quit the flattery or I am not marrying you.'

Ethan nodded and joined her in facing Matthew, who was rubbing his chin as he stared at each of them in turn.

'Usually,' he murmured, 'I say a few words first about—'

'Just do it!' Amelia said. 'And afterwards, do not invite the groom to kiss the bride or I will do something most unladylike.'

Matthew gulped, then hurried outside to drag in the first person he could find as a witness. Then he proceeded to wed them with the most haste he could muster.

Throughout the process, Ethan felt the mix of humour and tension that had fuelled him since he'd had this mad idea evaporate, and a solemnity that he hadn't expected overcame him. He guessed he was remembering his previous marriages, but he fought down those feelings and responded in a voice that he heard as being gruff.

Amelia, too, responded in a serious manner, and when the process was over Matthew turned and busied himself with the paperwork, while Ethan strapped on his gun, then paced to the window to stare out into the road.

'Forgive me, Martha,' he whispered to himself, then noticed that Amelia was standing beside him. He glanced at her, but whether she had heard him, he couldn't tell as she looked at him with that determined look which had overcome her every time they'd faced danger.

He flashed her a smile, receiving one, then looked into the road.

'Now,' Matthew said, 'you two love . . . you two people, do you want to stay the night with me? Sarah can make up a—'

'We will stay here,' Amelia said.

'My house will be more comfortable.'

'It will, but once the word gets out, there may be trouble, and I'd prefer you not to be involved. If nothing happens tonight, I don't think it ever will.'

'Then I'll look in on you later, if you don't mind.'

'Why would we mind?' Amelia turned to face Matthew, her wide-eyed gaze defying him to make an improper comment, but Matthew just coughed and headed to the door.

They watched him pace across the road. Then Ethan searched for the best place to sleep for the night. He settled down behind the desk, figuring he'd avoid any draughts while being in a position to watch the door.

Amelia padded around the room, her gaze darting over all the places in which Ethan had considering settling down, with the added incentive of searching for a place away from him. But she eventually settled down between Ethan and the wall so that she was hidden from anyone looking through the window or coming through the door.

'Don't worry,' Ethan said, 'you'll be safe there.'

'I know that.'

'And try to get some sleep.'

'I will.' She coughed. 'And, Ethan?'

'Yes.'

'We may be married, but if you come within four feet of me, I will kill you.'

'Yes, dear,' Ethan murmured.

CHAPTER 15

'I got to ask you something,' Ethan said, then coughed and looked through the window.

Ethan had been a married man for three hours. It had been a silent time and, against all his expectations, he'd done a lot of thinking, then some pacing, then some more thinking. And now a growing desire to do something even more stupid than offering to marry Amelia was overcoming him.

'About what?' Amelia asked, sitting up and leaning back against the wall.

Ethan turned to place his back to the window.

'About what we do now.'

'I expect everyone will know soon enough.' She smoothed her wedding-dress over her legs. 'And we'll find out if Seth and Cullen will put up a fight soon enough, too.'

'I didn't mean about that.'

'Then what?'

Ethan closed his eyes, wishing he'd never broached a subject that he should have kept quiet.

'Us,' he whispered.

'There is no *us*. We may be married but that means nothing.'

'I know, but we've been getting on well for the last few days and . . .' Ethan watched Amelia's mouth fall open, then tipped back his hat. 'Oh, forget it.'

Amelia rolled to her knees, then stood. 'Are you asking me what I think you're asking me?'

Ethan couldn't meet her gaze and turned to look through the window, then breathed a sigh of relief and pointed.

'Your lawyer friend is coming back to the office.'

'Forget him. Are you really asking me whether we could ever be married, in all the senses of the word?'

Ethan stared at the advancing Matthew, willing him to speed up and cut off the worst conversation he'd ever initiated in his life. But Matthew stopped to talk to someone in the middle of the road, and he had no choice but to turn and face her.

'I guess I'm wondering whether it's completely impossible that we could ever be married, and that's different.'

'It is different.' Amelia took a steady pace towards him. 'And I guess nothing is completely impossible. But when you said you wanted to marry me, you said you wouldn't hold me to anything.'

'And I won't. I don't want your ranch.'

'You might not, but you didn't say: "I don't want you." '

'Forget this,' Ethan said, glancing into the road and seeing that Matthew was now heading towards the office. 'I'm just trying to make sense of a situation I've never faced before.'

'And so am I. And I need to know what you're asking me.'

'I . . . I . . .'

The door swung open and Matthew strode in. He looked at each of them in turn, his eyes narrowing as he probably detected the tension between them, then shrugged.

'Everyone knows,' he declared.

'How?' Amelia asked, her gaze still on Ethan.

'I might have let it slip in the Silver Horseshoe.'

'And what did everyone say?'

'Everyone is just pleased a wedding's happened.' Matthew rocked his head from side to side. 'And I don't know who'll be the first to come here and tell you what they really think about it. But it won't be long.'

Ethan pointed through the window. 'And I got bad news. That first person is Wesley. And I don't reckon he's coming to congratulate us.'

'I'll deal with him,' Amelia said, walking towards the door.

Ethan stood to the side to block her way.

'You've already dealt with him at your wedding. I'll speak to him.'

'You will do no such thing. Until you tell me what your intentions are, I will not accept you ordering me about.' She flared her eyes. 'And not even then.'

Matthew stood back, peering at them, but before Ethan could even think of answering, Wesley staggered in. A gale of whiskey breath heralded his attitude as he took two belligerent paces towards Ethan, then swayed to a halt and pointed a shaking, half-empty bottle of whiskey in Ethan's general direction.

'You double-crossing varmint,' he shouted, slurring every word.

'You're worse for drink, again,' Ethan said, keeping his voice level. 'Just leave.'

'I ain't leaving until I've taught you a lesson.'

Wesley waved his arms for balance, tottered back two paces, then thrust his head down and stumbled across the room. He swayed to a halt five feet short of Ethan. He teetered another pace, then threw a punch at him that missed by two feet, but it did swing Wesley round to throw his hat from his head and land him on his knees. He stared at the floor, breathing in damp drags of breath.

Ethan moved to help him to his feet, but Wesley lunged his shoulders, throwing his hands away from him, and stumbled to his feet to stand with his legs planted wide and the bottle of whiskey dangling in his grasp.

'Just go,' Amelia said, her voice small and concerned.

'I ain't going until Ethan's heard this.' Wesley waved the bottle at Ethan, sloshing a fountain of whiskey around him. He stared at the spilt drink with a flash of hurt in his eyes, then focused on Ethan. 'You . . . You . . . You just take care of her. She's precious.'

With that sudden end to his belligerence, Wesley fought back a· sob, then threw back his head and glugged the remaining contents of the whiskey into his open mouth. Then he swirled round and hurled the bottle at the wall for it to explode in a shower of glass.

141

With a lunging swoop, he grabbed his hat from the floor then set it straight on his head and, with what appeared to be an attempt at a dignified walk, snaked his way to the door. He lurched into the door-frame as he staggered out, then weaved across the road towards the saloon.

'He will be all right, won't he?' Amelia murmured.

Both Ethan and Matthew looked at her, but Matthew sighed and followed Wesley out.

'I'll make sure he comes to no harm,' he said.

Amelia bit her bottom lip as she watched Matthew leave, then turned to Ethan, who looked back at her, hoping that Wesley's interruption had driven all memory of their previous conversation from her mind.

'Will he get over this?' she asked.

'He will, and I hope he comes out of it as a better man.'

'He *was* a better man, but I don't know why he fell so far. Perhaps if I hadn't have gone away, things would have been different.'

'Perhaps.'

Amelia glanced through the window, watching Wesley lurch back into the Silver Horseshoe, then turned to Ethan.

'But that still leaves your question, and I still don't know exactly what it was you were asking me.'

Ethan winced. He looked through the window, hoping that someone else would come to the office and distract him from having to answer a question he'd initiated, but now wished he'd left as a mad idea. But he saw nobody aside from Matthew following Wesley into the saloon, so he turned.

Then a sudden movement caught his eye outside.

He swirled back to see a rider hurtle past the saloon, stopping only to reach down and grab Matthew, who flailed his arms to fight off the rider, but a firm rap on the head knocked him to his knees.

'Trouble outside,' Ethan said, and hurried to the door.

'I hope you aren't just trying to avoid answering my question.'

Ethan threw open the door, but stopped in the doorway.

'I am, but there's still trouble. Stay here and don't come out.'

He dashed outside and across the road. Outside the saloon, a wagon had pulled up and two men were rolling Matthew into the back. Ethan drew his gun and fired high to attract their attention, but they ignored him, leapt on to the front of the wagon, then hurried it down the road.

The rider stayed back long enough for Ethan to see that it was Seth, who fired a high slug that whistled ten feet over Ethan's head as a warning, then stood outside the saloon as the wagon hurried away. He and Ethan shared eye contact. Then Seth yanked the reins to the side and galloped after the wagon.

Despite the gunfire, nobody emerged from the saloon, leaving Ethan to turn and dash back to the office. Why they had taken Matthew, he didn't know, but he judged that chasing after them on his own wasn't as urgent as protecting Amelia.

He scurried through the door and slammed it shut behind him.

'You any idea why they want him?' he asked.

He waited for an answer, but when one didn't come he turned, to see that the room was deserted. The desk was lying on its side and trapped beneath one corner was a shredded length of Amelia's wedding-dress.

Ethan found no trace of the route Amelia's kidnappers had taken, and this left him forlornly to search White Creek, then head out of town and search along the main trails. He found no trace of either her or Matthew.

He even tried the Bar J ranch, but he needed to get everyone out of bed. Worse, Frank refused to believe his boys were capable of doing wrong and threatened to kill him if he didn't leave the ranch immediately. Ethan left, taking Frank's attitude to be that of a wronged father and not an accomplice.

With all avenues blocked, he considered heading to the law office in Rawbone, but that journey would take until long after sun-up, and he figured that by then, there wouldn't be a problem left to solve.

When he returned to stand on White Creek's main road, the only lights glowing in town were in the saloon. And the only possibility of finding her came to him.

He went into the Silver Horseshoe. Only a few of the hardest drinkers were still there, all too bleary-eyed even to notice him arrive, but he was only interested in the man lying sprawled over the bar.

He stood beside him, then lifted the man's head to peer into his half-closed and red eyes.

'What you want?' Wesley slurred.

'Amelia's gone.'

'I know that, and I lost her.'

'I mean she's gone. Your brothers have taken her.'

'You took her. You married her for yourself. You ain't no—'

'Listen to me,' Ethan roared. He grabbed Wesley's jacket and stood him straight, then shook his shoulders, the force rocking his head back and forth. 'Your brothers have kidnapped Amelia and I'm sure they mean her harm. What you say to that?'

Ethan stopped shaking him and stared into his rolling eyes.

Wesley heaved. 'I want to be sick.'

Ethan stared down at him, but when Wesley heaved, he pushed him away. Wesley fell to his knees and tried to vomit up everything he'd ever eaten in his whole life. But Ethan stood over him and when the heaving stopped, he pulled him to his feet and dragged him to a chair by the door. He ensured he was receiving a cooling breeze, then went to the stove, but he had to search around until he found the coffee-pot on the floor.

The pot was ice-cold. He looked inside to see that a scummy green fur had grown over the murky contents, but he decided they would be good enough to start Wesley off on the sobering-up process. He poured him a mug, then paced back across the saloon and thrust it in his hand.

As Wesley stared at the evil-smelling dregs, Ethan

ordered the bartender to rinse out the pot, then start a good thick brew going.

He returned to find Wesley gulping down a mouthful of the festering coffee. Then Wesley spat it out in a huge spout and fell to his knees to embark on a second round of heaving. Ethan waited until he'd finished, then dragged him back into his chair.

'Had enough?'

'I want to die,' Wesley murmured.

'You ain't got time, because you're about to sober up. Then you're going to start thinking where Amelia might have gone.'

Wesley looked up. 'Amelia's gone?'

Ethan sighed. 'This is going to be a long night.'

Two pots of coffee didn't exactly sober up Wesley, but it did get him through several more sessions of heaving and a lengthy bemoaning of all the mistakes he'd made in his life.

Ethan let him wallow in his misfortune, but from the fragments he did listen to, he gathered that his first impressions were correct. So, when Wesley's eyes were relatively clear, he relented from tormenting him with thicker and thicker slugs of coffee and smiled for the first time.

'You trying to tell me you still got feelings for Amelia, then?'

'More than you have,' Wesley snarled.

'Perhaps, but you didn't act like you cared for her last night.'

Wesley swirled his mug. 'I guess I didn't.'

'And who told you that acting like that was the right thing to do?'

'I ain't had much advice as to what I should do around womenfolk. Father never spent much time with my mother, and Seth and Cullen reckoned that enjoying myself with saloon-girls was the right thing to do.'

'For them it might have been, but not when you got a woman like Amelia.'

Wesley slammed the mug on the table, then slapped it to the floor.

'I know that now. I just wish it was yesterday.' Wesley fought back a sob, then buried his face in his hands. 'But it ain't, and now you're married to her.'

'That's just a convenience to get over the problem with her father's will. I'm no husband, and neither are you unless you change.'

Wesley looked up, a flash of cheer lightening his eyes.

'You reckon you can persuade her to talk to me and put things right?'

'It'll take years to put things right, if ever, but we got to worry about the first problem first. And that's finding her.'

Wesley shook his head. 'But I don't know where anyone would take Amelia. And I can't believe my brothers would want to harm her.'

'Then perhaps they ain't as vicious as I thought. Perhaps they hired Buck Lincoln to kidnap her, but that man wanted his own revenge. Perhaps they're now trying to force her to sign away the ranch to them and they need the lawyer to make it legal.' Ethan shrugged. 'So, think, where could they have taken her?'

'I can't think.'

Ethan grabbed the coffee-pot and waved it towards the bartender.

'Get more coffee,' he shouted. 'And double the strength again.'

Wesley raised a hand. 'I can't face no more of that.'

Ethan slammed the pot down before Wesley.

'Until you're sober enough to think where she is, I'm feeding you coffee. And I won't stop until you explode.'

Wesley gulped. 'In that case, perhaps I do have an idea.'

CHAPTER 16

'Why this place?' Ethan asked.

Wesley pulled his horse to a halt beside the ramshackle sod-house.

'This is where my father and Amelia's father first settled the area.'

'And what reason you got to suppose they're here beside it stopping me feeding you raw coffee?'

'Seth sometimes stays here when he's fallen out with Father, which is often.'

'Then that's good enough for me.'

Ethan nudged his horse forward to approach the house.

The moon was up and large, but scudding clouds reduced the light and Ethan could only just make out the outline of the house. But as they approached, he reckoned he heard at least one horse whinnying and this was enough for him to dismount and, with Wesley at his side, run towards the house, keeping low.

They hunkered down beside a short length of fence at an angle where they could peer through the open doorway and inside. And there, Ethan was sure he detected a glow. He gave silent orders to Wesley to head to the side of the house then crawl beneath the only window to get to the door.

Wesley nodded and stood, but then Seth leapt up into the window and fired a slug at them. It was high and meant as a warning, but it still forced both men to throw themselves to the ground and lie flat.

'Go away!' Seth shouted from the house.

'This is Ethan Craig. And I have Wesley with me. This is over.'

'Go, while you still can.'

'You can't speak to your brother like that,' Wesley shouted.

Silence was the only response they got, and despite a flashed glare from Ethan, Wesley rolled to his knees and moved to stand.

But then Seth fired at them again, forcing Wesley to drop to the ground beside Ethan, then duck.

'They ain't in the mood for listening to sense,' Ethan whispered. 'Let me take care of this.'

'This is my family and my family's problem.'

'It ain't. They got my wife in there.'

Wesley's eyes flashed with something more than just annoyance, but he nodded and Ethan crawled past the corral fence, working his way forwards with his elbows. Wesley stayed back, but when Ethan was a good ten feet ahead of him, he leapt to his feet.

'I've stood,' he shouted. 'And no matter what's at stake here, you won't kill me. So, I'm walking towards the house and we'll talk this out.'

A man appeared at the window and peered out as

Wesley paced towards the house, but Ethan winced, then darted a glance over his shoulder.

'Get down,' he shouted.

'That's my kin in there.'

'They are, but that man ain't one of them.'

Wesley did a double-take, then peered into the darkened house, but the man at the window levelled a gun on him. In desperate self-preservation, Wesley hurled himself to the ground to lie flat. Lead hurtled by the spot where he'd been standing, and a second slug whistled over his falling form.

But from the ground, Ethan tore a quick shot into the man's chest that stood him straight, before he stumbled and toppled forwards to lie dangling over the window frame.

Barked orders and recriminations ripped out from the house, but Ethan gestured to Wesley to use the momentary confusion to head for the side of the door. Then he jumped up and dashed for the wall with Wesley at his heels.

Another man edged into the doorway and fired a shot that plumed into the earth at Ethan's feet, but Wesley caught the man with a glancing blow to the arm that toppled him into the side of the doorway.

On the run, Ethan tore a shot into the man's side that slid him to the ground to lie still. Before the brothers could make a move, he reached the building and pressed himself flat beside the door.

Wesley arrived a moment later and stood on the other side of the door.

'I guess those men were what's left of Buck Lincoln's group,' Ethan shouted. 'You made a big mistake getting involved with him.'

'You don't give the orders here,' Seth shouted from deep within the house.

'We're brothers,' Wesley said from the other side of the doorway. 'Those men didn't care about that, but we do. We can talk this out.'

From inside, Cullen urged Seth to listen, but Seth beat back his pleas with a curt command.

'Brother or no brother,' Seth shouted. 'I'll shoot the first man that comes through that door.'

Wesley moved to go in anyhow, but Ethan shook his head. Wesley nodded and shouted another request, but Ethan used the distraction to dive through the door, keeping low. He rolled over his shoulder as he came to rest lying on his side five feet in from the door. Even in the poor light, he saw Matthew and Amelia sitting by the back wall with Cullen standing over them and Seth standing in the middle of the room.

He bobbed up to slam a high shot into Cullen's shoulder, which wheeled him away. Wesley followed him in and trained his gun down on the wounded man, but Seth dashed back two paces and grabbed Amelia's arm. He yanked her to her feet and swung her round to hold her from behind, then slammed his gun against her neck.

'Stop!' Wesley shouted, skidding to a halt and raising his hands. 'I didn't want to believe you planned to hurt Amelia. Up until now I thought it was Buck's idea to kill her, but unless you put that gun down, one of us will kill you.'

'We worked her father's ranch for the last five

years. She's done nothing. We deserve that land.'

'You deserve nothing. Now release her.'

'Brother, you ain't ordering me around.'

'Then listen to me,' Ethan said. 'You can still walk away from this with a prison sentence, but the moment you pull that trigger, you ain't the only one who'll die.'

'I don't believe that.' Seth gripped Amelia's shoulder and dragged her in to stand pressed tight against him. He held her against his chest and something in the whiteness of his knuckles suggested to Ethan how this whole sorry episode had started.

He nodded to himself then, with his gun trained down at the floor, stood and faced Seth.

'Then perhaps Amelia was wrong about you.'

'What?' Seth snapped.

'Over the last few days we've spent a lot of time together, and we talked a-plenty. She told me she thought you were the more handsome brother, and she wished she could have married you.'

Wesley whined and Amelia's eyes opened wide, but when she saw Ethan's wide-eyed stare, she gave a short nod.

'Really?' Seth murmured. He released his grip of Amelia's shoulder and pulled the gun from her neck, then turned her to look into her eyes. 'You could have been my bride?'

'And not just a bride,' she said, her voice soft as she folded her arms, burying her hands deep in her wedding dress. Then gunmetal flashed as she pulled out her hand and in a moment, she'd slapped a gun up tight beneath his chin. 'I'm a six-shooter bride.'

With a sharp movement, Seth darted his head back from the gun. Ethan and Wesley broke into a run, both yelling at her to dive to the floor, but Amelia swirled round and, with a round-armed slap of her other hand, flattened Seth's nose.

Seth staggered back, his knees buckling, but the raised knee Amelia delivered to him finished the buckling and he collapsed, his eyes rolling.

And when he stopped writhing, it was to find that Ethan and Wesley were standing over him with their guns trained down on him.

'Did she really say that?' Wesley asked from the corner of his mouth.

'No,' Ethan said, then dragged Seth to his feet. 'Nobody could love this varmint.'

Ethan checked that Matthew was composed enough to hold a gun on their prisoners, while Wesley offered to help Amelia leave the house, but she rebuffed him and left the house with her head held high. Ethan prepared to follow her out, then noticed the slew of papers on a table by the side wall.

He checked with Matthew and confirmed that Seth hadn't been able to force Amelia to sign anything. Even so, he stayed behind to rip the papers into shreds.

He also found a clean sheet of paper, which he folded into an envelope, then slotted the envelope into his pocket. Only then did he follow everyone outside.

CHAPTER 17

Standing before the house, Ethan considered his prisoners and decided that Wesley could escort the wounded Cullen into town to get his shoulder fixed. But he decided to take Seth and the two dead hardcases to the law office in Rawbone, figuring that he now needed the help of the law to resolve the frayed ends of this situation.

Amelia stood back from the house with her gun on Seth while Ethan threw the dead men over their horses. Ethan then drew Wesley aside and, with his back turned to Amelia, gave him the envelope.

'Keep this letter safe,' he said, keeping his voice low so that only Wesley could hear him. 'When you think you're ready, give it to Amelia.'

'What does it say?' Wesley asked.

'I can't do no reading or writing so it's a blank sheet of paper, but I want you to write a letter from a friend telling Amelia that I'm dead.'

Wesley blinked hard. 'But why?'

'Because then she'll be a widow, and you and her . . .'

'You don't have to do this.'

Ethan sighed. 'Ours wasn't a real marriage, and we have to sort it out somehow. That'll take care of any loose ends.'

'I guess it will.' Wesley glanced at Amelia, who was now standing with Matthew and still looking away from him. 'But I reckon it'll take many a year for her to forgive me.'

'I reckon so, too, but if you want her to do that bad enough, you'll do it.'

'I will. I promise you that.' Wesley flashed a smile. 'If only to stop someone like you forcing coffee down my throat.'

'You'd better, because dead man or no dead man, if I ever find out you ain't, I'll come back and see you. And I won't waste my time on no coffee or on no haunting, if you understand me.'

'I reckon I do.' Wesley tipped his hat, but their low tones had enticed Amelia to join them.

'What are you talking about?' she asked, looking at Ethan.

'About what we should tell everyone,' Ethan said. 'And Wesley says we should admit the full truth, even if it ruins his family's good name.'

'That was the right decision.' Amelia glanced at Ethan's horse. 'And I guess you're getting the law in.'

'I am.'

'Then hurry back.' She smiled. 'We have much to discuss.'

'I won't be coming back.'

'But . . .' Amelia glanced at Wesley, who had the grace to back away and leave them, then busy himself with ensuring that Seth was secure on his horse.

'I think it's for the best,' Ethan said.

'Perhaps, but what about all those things you said?'

'I said nothing.'

'You nearly said plenty.'

'That was just me musing, but if I'd have thought for even a moment, I wouldn't have said anything.'

'But I'm glad you did.' She laid a hand on his arm. 'And I really would like to hear the question that you so nearly asked me.'

Ethan looked skywards, watching the moon slip out from behind a cloud and for one long moment, he imagined himself saying something; then he shook his head.

'Amelia,' he said, shrugging his arm away, 'you and I got pretty close for the last few days, but let's not continue the mistake.'

'Perhaps it is a mistake, but we'll never work out if it is a mistake if you go.' She placed her hand on his, and in the coolness of the night, it burnt his skin.

Ethan took a deep breath. 'You're right, but you and Wesley were apart for five years and you still worked out that he was right for you.'

'And how wrong I was,' she snapped, flashing a harsh glare at Wesley.

'You might not be.' Ethan lifted her hand from his, enjoying her last touch, then turned to his horse. 'But I still got business down south with my family to attend to. So, I reckon this is another test.'

'So, you will come back?'

Ethan mounted his horse. He looked back to check that Wesley had secured Seth, then turned to look down at Amelia.

'Yeah. Once I've seen my kin, I'll swing back this way later in the year and you'll have had time to think. And if you still think it's worth me asking that question, I'll ask it.'

She nodded and shrugged her dress to play it out around her.

'Then I'll see you later in the year.'

Ethan stared down at her, enjoying looking at a woman who was only his wife because they were married, then tore his gaze away to look towards Rawbone. Ahead was a woman who was once his wife but didn't want him. Behind was a woman who was his wife but might just want him.

He glanced at Wesley and at the envelope he had withdrawn from his pocket and was holding up to him while miming tearing it in half. Ethan tried to shake his head, but found that he couldn't move, then glanced down at Amelia again.

'Later in the year,' he said, then hurried away into the night.